F
HANSC
Quest
1st e

24 M
-5 J'
1
1:

QUEST

QUEST

VIC J. HANSON

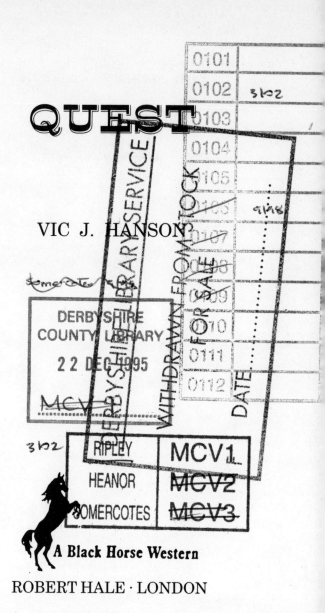

A Black Horse Western

ROBERT HALE · LONDON

© Vic J. Hanson 1995
First published in Great Britain 1995

ISBN 0 7090 5732 6

Robert Hale Limited
Clerkenwell House
Clerkenwell Green
London EC1R 0HT

Photoset in North Wales by
Derek Doyle & Associates, Mold, Clwyd.
Printed and bound in Great Britain by
WBC Book Manufacturers Limited,
Bridgend, Mid-Glamorgan.

1

'If that's what you want to do, Obe,' said Cracker. 'It isn't up to me to try and dissuade you.'

'Dissuade!' cried the other man, taller, younger. 'What kind of lingo is that?'

'For Pete's sake,' said Cracker. 'Can't you be serious for one peckin' minute?'

'Serious? An' use words like dissuade, huh?'

'I give up!' exploded Cracker, throwing gnarled hands in the air. 'Sometimes I think you haven't got any commonsense at all.'

'Quit talkin' like a judge.'

'It's a habit hard to break,' said the wizened veteran with the steel-rimmed spectacles and the old-style walrus moustache.

He began to fill his pipe like he mostly did when he was nervous. He didn't light it, just stuck the end in his mouth and sucked. He didn't smoke much nowadays anyway.

The younger man spoke again. 'I've got to find him, you know that.' He sounded serious now.

'I guess you have. But what're you going to do if

and when you find him?'

'I'll meet up with him all right, sooner or later. Then what is to happen will happen, I guess.'

'Now you're being cryptic.'

'There you go again!'

As things turned out though, it didn't take him as long to reach his man as he'd figured it might. The man, a gambler, kept moving where the money was.

The seeking rider was tall, rawboned, almost gaunt with a long face, thick red-gold hair, eyes that were blue and steady – very steady.

In a small outlaw town called Lobo Forks the seeking rider spotted a badly printed yellow poster tacked to a wall in a low-roofed cantina. A dirty place. Not a place to find quality. But gaming took place here at a big table in a corner, the only spot where the sun shone in.

This was a wide-open town and the clientele of this place was mostly of the lawless breed. Often well-britched too though. *Mucho dinero* changed hands here at the turn of a card.

The yellow poster had nothing to do with this kind of gambling, but gambling there would be at the advertised event, a fisticuff tournament run by one Elias 'Mad Boy' Slack.

Elias was no longer a boy, and he wasn't nearly as mad as he used to be. He had never been bested, however, and had only given up personally practising the manly art of self-defence when, ironically, he had been thrown by a horse in a lonely place.

The beast had been worse off than he and he'd had to shoot it. Then he'd had to crawl till he'd been picked up by a travelling drummer with a decent gig and a smart trotting pony.

Elias's shoulder was busted. It never healed properly. He turned to fight-promoting and ran a stable of tough young bucks who'd take on all-comers, bare-knuckle or wrestle.

At the trestle bar in the low-roofed cantina a voice said, 'Howdy, Obe', and the tall, dusty rider looked down upon a younker with the face of an angel.

'Howdy, Crip.'

'Didn't expect to see you in these parts, Obe.'

'Why not?'

'Oh, I dunno....'

The wide-eyed boyish face suddenly took on an uneasy look, even maybe a scared one.

The other man pointed a long finger at the yellow poster and asked, 'Where's that at?'

'I'll – I'll guide you if you like.'

'No need. Tell me.'

'All right, Obe.' The angel-faced younker called Crip pointed a finger himself now, chattered, gesticulated.

He watched the tall man called Obe walk from the place.

Others also watched the tall, flame-haired man, and an old-timer in a corner got up and crossed to the bar and said, 'He's a useful-lookin' cuss, Crip, an' I've got a sneaking idee I've seen him someplace before. Who is he?'

Before the small young man could answer, another man at the bar spoke up.

'I know who he is. That's Obadiah Quest.'

'Is that right?'

'It is,' put in Crip, who still looked a mite uneasy.

'Well, I guess he wasn't after you anyway, little pard,' said the old-timer. At the back of the two of them the know-all barfly laughed harshly as if he still knew something the old-timer didn't. But he said no more.

By this time Obadiah Quest had unhitched his horse from the rail outside the cantina. He mounted. He rode purposefully but not too fast, loose in the saddle atop the gaunt grey who seemed to match his rider. Folks gazed at them as they passed.

'That's Obadiah Quest,' said somebody; and somebody else said, 'I wonder if he's after a feller or two.'

'Usually is.'

The horse and rider passed out of their sight in the heat-haze and were soon loosely mingling with other travellers going in the same direction, some of them faster than others, as if in eagerness.

2

There was s sizeable crowd in the small valley with the slopes almost completely clear of vegetation. Folks were ranked on the greensward, their livestock grazing nearby and gigs, wagons and suchlike on the flats behind.

There was a rocky patch halfway on one slope, activity there, oily, brown flesh glistening in the sunlight.

Quest steered his grey towards this spot and, as he did so, a figure came out to meet him: a big misshapen man with one lumpy shoulder higher than the other forming a sort of hump; thick neck topped by a moon face; small twinkling eyes surrounded by scar tissue.

Quest slid from the saddle and the other man caught him in a bearlike embrace, crying gutturally, 'Obe, by all that's holy!'

'Howdy, Elias.'

The humped giant backed off a little but didn't let go, gripped Quest's shoulders and held him at arm's length.

'You had the nose fixed.'

'Doc in Tombstone,' said Quest. 'Sorta pummelled it an' taped it. I looked like a clown for a couple weeks. Fixed my breathin' though – it was beginnin' to bother me some.'

'Yeh, I know. This game wasn't for you, Obe. I allus said you could do better than this. And you have I guess.'

'It's a moot point.' That's what old Cracker might've said, Quest reflected. Retired Judge Cracker who, Quest knew, still valued the friendship of such as he, a notorious gunfighter, and would've been glad to learn that another old friend, Elias 'Mad Boy' Slack was still very much alive, if not kicking in the way he used to.

'Remember young Jigger?' Elias asked.

'Sure do. He still with you?'

'Sure is. My prime boy. He's got a big one agin him today, ready to start any minute now.'

Quest hadn't even had time to greet young Jigger who hadn't changed much, looked at the peak of fitness. He was already pacing into the middle of the improvised arena to meet his opponent who, it seemed, was called Pecos George.

George looked like an ape.

Both men were stripped to the waist, had only pants belted tightly. They were barefooted. Jigger's muscular torso was almost hairless.

Pecos George, however, was literally smothered with shaggy black hair, except for his pig-like face which was as bare as most of his pink head, with

only what looked like a ball of fluff over each
bat-like ear.

Elias Slack dropped one of his ham-like hands
in a sort of chopping motion. That was all the
signal needed.

Now George's apelike aspect became even more
marked.

He half-crouched, light on his feet. His
half-curled hands dangled past his knees. He was
wide-open.

Jigger moved swiftly on his toes, topping his
man now by inches. A tight-faced young man with
brush-cropped black hair whose fists moved like
twin rapiers in the hands of an expert swordsman.

But they weren't fast enough – and a great
'Ah-aaagh' went up from the crowd.

It was Pecos George who had struck the first
blow.

Open was George's way, a come-on – then the
gap was closed with lightning speed. One hand
and a crooked arm blocking Jigger's blows,
one-two. And George's other fist going up and
over, whipping like a hammer and smashing into
the bridge of Jigger's nose.

The boy didn't have a big nose: it looked sort of
boneless. It wasn't *bloodless* though, and as its
owner staggered backwards the claret burst from
it like a small red fountain splashing in the bright
sun.

After that Jigger didn't stand a chance as
George went after him, into him. Not like an ape
now or a grizzly bear but like a fighting, killing

machine, pumping and grunting until Jigger lay motionless on his face in the dust.

Elias Slack rolled the unconscious boy over, inspected him anxiously. Obadiah Quest joined him, both of them on one knee.

'His face,' ejaculated Elias. 'Obe, his nose is busted. And it looks like a jaw. And hell knows what else.'

'I'll take over,' said Quest, straightening up.

'You're out of training, man.'

'Watch me.'

The tall, long-faced man with the flaming red-gold hair was soon down to his pants. He sat down and pulled off his riding boots while the stolid, ape-like figure of Pecos George stood waiting.

Two men came forth to carry young Jigger away. Elias stepped back and, with one resigned look at his friend Obadiah, raised his hand aloft. But still he held it poised.

Quest looked at Pecos George and said, 'You ready, big man?'

'I'm ready, tall man.'

The hairy giant's mouth split in a snaggle-toothed grin and for a moment he looked harmless, even likeable. But that didn't cause Quest to sell him short at all, *nossir*. He had seen George treat young Jigger like a rag doll and literally throw him away.

Elias's hand fell. The two opponents were both fast, deceptively fast, particularly George, who looked like a hairy lump on legs

Quest feinted with a left, whipped a right across. But George was ready for that: his fist smashed the right aside, went through it, aiming at the full of Quest's long face. Only the slight jerk of the rawboned man's head saved him and even then the meaty pad grazed his ear.

Then Quest crouched a little: he thrust a fist at George's meaty middle, which carried more than a mite of adiposity. And the powerful blow sank home.

The giant went 'Woof' and Quest caught a blast of his breath and that wasn't pleasant at all. Then, bent forward from the blow as George was, he managed to ram a fist into Quest's shoulder, spinning him.

George was a practised roughhouse man; he knew all the tricks and didn't waste any time at all. He fought by instinct, but with a kind of finesse also. He let his momentum carry him on after his adversary as, coming out of his spin, Quest was backing a little.

The last blow had momentarily paralyzed his left shoulder. He flexed that arm and shooting pains hit the shoulder and he was ready again and both fists came up as he evaded George, circled him.

George spun around, one fist up, one down. The guard covered his hairy torso pretty well. But the swift-moving Quest found a gap.

He used his fist like a hammer which smashed into the big feller's cheekbone, splitting it, knocking him on his butt as blood burst from the wound.

Quest could've stomped him then. Some of the crowd would've loved that. But he backed off a little and didn't hit the big man again until George was on his feet but wasn't properly balanced. You didn't give a fighting machine like this one too much leeway, though.

A right, a left. And George was down once more. But soon risen again, maybe too quickly, and Quest going in to him again, fists pumping like twin pistons.

Now it was mayhem, with Pecos George backing mostly, though getting a blow in of his own from time to time. But Quest was slowly and deliberately cutting him down.

George went flat once more. But still he got up again as if he were on springs and, for a second, Quest didn't seem to be even looking at his adversary, was staring at the crowd. Or at somebody in particular among the crowd.

George swung. As if by instinct the tall man ducked under the blow and retaliated with a right on the button which propelled George backwards, and flat again as if he'd been kicked by an angry horse.

Quest leapt over the prone form and charged at the crowd. He burst through them and out the other side, free except for stragglers who hastened to get out of his way. They had already been scattered by a man on a horse who rode his beast as if the Devil was on his tail.

Obadiah Quest grabbed a saddleless cayuse that just happened to be in the way. A fast-looking paint who had more than a smidgen of Injun in him. He went off at a half-bucking tangent as if he'd been suddenly bitten in the ass by a sidewinder.

He hit a small wagon sideways and his new and unwelcome rider was precipitated from the smooth back on to a pile of farming implements which did his half-naked anatomy no good at all.

Swearing, Quest got up, and the paint pranced away delightedly.

The tall man got down from the wagon. He was bleeding in a few places but not too badly he thought. Elias Slack approached him, said, 'That was – that rider, that was Buck Beckon.'

'I know.'

'But why...?'

Quest interrupted, saying flatly, 'He was responsible for the death of my father.'

That's a funny way to put it, thought Elias. But he said nothing more right then, turned back towards the crowd, a row of staring faces.

3

Pecos George was on his feet, swaying a little, bleary-eyed. When he saw Quest he sat down on a pile of saddles. He looked up at the tall man out of one good eye, the other being temporarily closed.

'You beat me fair an' square, tall man,' he said.

'It was a good fight,' said Quest. 'And one of the hardest I've ever had, an' that's the truth.'

Pecos George looked at Elias 'Mad Boy' Slack, asked, 'How's the boy?'

'He'll be all right. He's lyin' down in the wagon.'

George grinned his snaggle-toothed grin. 'An' I ain't fightin' anybody else today.'

'I ain't askin' you to.'

'I'm goin' back to town an' the little woman.'

The thought of this hairy giant having a 'little woman' was somewhat ludicrous, but it was the truth, as Elias affirmed to his friend Obe later.

And, right then, Pecos George got himself dressed and mounted an old burro he called Hector who took him in a lopsided, ambling way until the strange cortège was almost lost in the

heat-haze, the town of Lobo Forks like a wispy
mirage ahead of them.

'I asked him to come with us, join the team,'
Elias said. 'But he runs a dry goods store in town,
would you believe that?'

'There are stranger things than a bruiser like
George runnin' a store,' said Quest with a wry
grin. 'I bet nobody messes with his produce
anyway.'

'Yeah, folks change,' said Elias, eyeing his tall
friend quizzically.

Quest didn't respond and Elias went on, 'You
get yourself cleaned up, bucko, while I go see
young Jigger. I didn't say anything to George, but
I didn't like the look of that young feller's jaw. We
sent for the doc from town. He might be here now.'

'Yeh, you go see,' said Quest.

There was a sort of first-aid station where lesser
casualties could get succour of a kind. Quest
washed up, salved his wounds (they didn't need
anything more than that) and got himself togged.
And all the time he was thinking, remembering.
This wasn't the first time he'd gone through this
first-aid process, not by a long sight.

He remembered so much now. He'd been a kid
who would fight anything that moved, and eat
some of it also. When he'd joined Elias's bunch the
big man had shown him how to soak his fists in
brine to make them as hard as hickory, how to
grease them if they got split or bruised – but
always the brine before and after and in-between
times, always that.

Quest had been lucky that he'd never suffered any bad damage to his hands. When he had given up using his fists for a living and had taken up a town marshal's post he had oiled those lean, fast-moving hands and they had continued to work well for him.

He had been a man behind a badge who did as he was paid to do: enforce the law. He had been forced into fights with lawbreakers and he had killed. His swift-moving hands had been like swords of justice.

But he had swift feet too. He was an inveterate fiddlefoot. He moved from town to town, took job after job. He didn't actually seek a rep as a fast gun, but he made one – and other fast guns began to seek him out. And soon it transpired that not many towns could risk a marshal who carried a rep like his. That was as likely to bring in other gunnies looking for a rep (I'm the jasper who kilt Obadiah Quest) instead of drive 'em away.

So Obadiah Quest, who purely hated the scum of the earth that seemed to be trying to take over the West and make it into their own image, became a bounty hunter – and his formidable killing reputation grew and grew....

In one town (a short spell of marshalling) he lived with a saloon girl for a while. A plump, black-haired beauty called Estelle. She had been crossing the street when she was hit by a stray bullet as trouble erupted out of swinging saloon doors. Her brain destroyed, she had died instantly. Quest had killed the two men who'd been responsible for the shooting. Then he had moved on, had kept moving on.

Then he made a long-overdue visit back home and something else happened. Something terrible....

But he didn't want to think about that any more now.

He'd had a chance – and he had blown that chance away....

Elias returned. 'You staying a while, Obe?' he asked.

'I'm goin' back to Lobo Forks anyway. How's Jigger?'

'The doc took him back to town in the gig. His jaw's got to be wired, an' other things are to be done. He won't fight again.'

'That's the game. Still, maybe Jigger's better off at that.'

There were no more fights. The one between Quest and Pecos George had been the last. Any more would have been an anticlimax. Folks were still talking about that final one.

'How are the hands?' Elias asked.

'They'll be all right.'

Elias looked as if he was about to say something else, maybe more questions. But whatever it was, he bottled it.

'You comin' into town?' Quest asked.

'I'll come in with you if you give me a little time to fix that things are shipshape here.'

'I'll ride,' said Quest flatly. 'I'll see you in town

later, huh?'

'Just as you wish, ol' pardner. You know the
Dirty Ace?'

'The saloon? Sure I do.'

'I'll see you there, huh?'

'I guess.'

'Hope you can make it.'

'Likewise.'

It was a sort of cryptic conversation which
didn't seem to mean a lot but could have meant a
whole lot more, but with not even the conversa-
tionalists quite knowing what that lot – or the
least of it – might be.

And one of them feeling somewhat peeved,
telling himself that he didn't know anything at
all, only suspected something; didn't know what
that was either and wasn't sure whether he
wanted to get the rights of it after all.

Elias 'Mad Boy' Slack. Watching his old friend
ride away into the sunset and wondering whether
he would see that lanky figure in town later after
all.

Obe wasn't riding a hastily borrowed mount
now but his own handsome grey stallion and they
went so well together; maybe they'd go right on
through. Maybe they'd be held up in town though.
There were reasons....

Elias didn't know what those reasons were. He
didn't want to lose sight of Obe so soon again. But
he worried....

He was getting to be a soft, werriting sort of old
cuss in his later years. Let it go, old son, he told

himself, Obe would do what he had to do (whatever that was), he always had.

Elias turned back to things in hand. Bets had been made and pay-offs were the order now. Money was changing hands. There were happy folk and there were disgruntled ones. Some had backed the local favourite Pecos George. They'd been paid off on the defeat of young Jigger. But Obadiah Quest as a prizefighter had been a surprise to all, a gunfighter who had to take care of his hands.

It had been a grand fight though, you had to admit that.

Now Elias 'Mad Boy' Slack worried about his old friend's hands. He'd wanted to inspect them after the fight. Quest had said they were all right.

Stop it, Elias told himself again, for Pete's sake stop it!

He was soon surrounded by people, and questions, compliments and suggestions were thrown at him. He and his boys had been going to move on but now, in a split second, Elias changed his plans, said they'd stay in this territory a while longer, maybe put on another show.

4

Lobo Forks wasn't a big town. It was bigger now than when Quest first remembered it. It seemed cleaner and less noisy.

Folks were already coming back from the fist tournaments. The gambling fraternity and hangers-on, and a few good-time girls of the kind who liked to watch men fight.

Not even as many of that kind of women, however, as there used to be, unless they were someplace else, fleecing the suckers in the saloon and in the gambling dens – or about their other business. There had been plenty of that other business in the old days.

This had been a real outlaw town that had had no law at all, had been in fact a bolthole for lawbreakers and a place for nefarious tradings.

The place had been virtually run by an immensely fat half-breed called merely Esteban who, Quest had recently learned, had been shot in the back one dark night while strolling round his house on the edge of town. Nobody had been spotted; nobody had been caught.

At that time Esteban had had living with him the angel-faced boy called Crip. But Crip said he'd been asleep in bed and had been awakened by the shot.

He had found Esteban dead on the porch to where he'd managed to crawl, leaving a trail of blood behind him. That was all Crip knew.

Crip was a scavenger, a jackal. He had been Esteban's jackal. In common with most people, Quest had figured that when Esteban died Crip had lost a meal ticket.

Or had he?

When Quest had seen the blue-eyed boy last, only that morning in the Dirty Ace Saloon, Crip hadn't seemed badly britched at all. So maybe he'd gotten himself another protector, another meal ticket.

Quest decided to visit the Dirty Ace again. Yeh, that was the ticket. And he wouldn't only be looking for Crip. That was a sad thought, but it was a thought that had to be faced, an action that had to be taken if that was the way it should be, had to be.

Crip was still there. He was uneasy at being asked questions. He put on a guileless face but his blue eyes were shifty. He had no answers. Quest decided not to press him too hard.

There was nobody else in the Dirty Ace that Quest wanted to talk to.

He left the place and began to range the town.

Crip had told him that there was now law of a

sort here, an elderly feller who called himself
'town constable' and practised lawyering as well.

Things were certainly looking up in Lobo Forks.

The feller was called Septimus Lagg. Quest
didn't know whether he wanted to see the feller or
not.

He passed the place; looked like the ground
floor of a boarding-house, a few rickety steps
leading up to the door, a shingle above it.
Septimus Lagg. That was the moniker all right.
And after the name, in brackets, one other word:
Law. That didn't mean a lot, did it? Quest
wondered what his old friend Judge Cracker, who
had a phrase for everything, would have to say
about that.

Quest turned off the cart-rutted, hoof-pocked
main street. The alleys each side – and there
seemed to be more than there used to be – were
too narrow to take any kind of vehicle except a
handcart. The tall man thought maybe he knew
this particular alley. There used to be a decent
cantina down here that did good stew. But he
wasn't hungry right now.

The cantina was still there, looked like the
same cadaverous man behind the bar. Just to be
neighbourly Quest took a shot of tequila with the
usual salt and lemon. The place wasn't very full.
He didn't see any other face he knew. The
bartender? Well, after a time all barkeeps tended
to look alike, something about the way they
handled themselves....

The gambling fraternity were back in town;

more of them drifted into the cantina, as they would in others along the alley. Quest moved on.

A well-shaped women with red hair and a gown with peacocks on it called him from the doorway of a crib.

'Later, honey,' he said, and wondered whether he meant that.

He found an establishment he was damn' sure he hadn't seen before – not in this town! A church. Or at least a building that had been turned into a place for praying, and maybe for singing also. Quest had a sneaking idea though that it had once been a whorehouse.

A small rickety-looking tower had been built upon it in which a small brass bell hung. Brown curtains wreathed the window at each side of the door. There were no red curtains, no red light shining in the dusk beyond. The wide door had been newly painted in a brilliant white.

The door was partially open but there was nobody around.

Quest couldn't see through the door. He did not approach it. Even so he felt that eyes were waching him. But not from the door, from the windows with the sun on them and the still curtains.

He turned his head. At the end of the alley a small figure flitted swiftly out of his view.

Was that angel-faced Crip?'

Was he following Quest and, if so, why? The jackal, the picker-up of unconsidered trifles.

Suddenly, though he didn't think anybody was

watching him any more, Quest grinned widely.
His teeth were white and unbroken in his long
face which mostly looked kind of saturnine. But
now momentarily that face lit up.

But the grin died: it always did. Lately he
hadn't had much to grin about. He was looking at
the church again.

It was still and nothing else moved.

He turned his head suddenly again, swiftly, as
if he were trying to catch somebody.

There was nobody there.

Maybe that little figure was hiding around the
corner. Or maybe, knowing it had been spotted, it
had scuttled away.

Did the figure have a gun?

To hell, thought Quest, and he certainly wasn't
even smiling now.

To hell.... We'll all go to hell, he thought. Folks
like me. A bullet in the back. Or a bullet in the
front.

He raised his feet one by one. He strode
purposefully forward again. He wasn't really sure
where he was going. The luck of the draw, he
thought, the turn of the card. And, with folks like
him, who knew what the next hour might bring –
or the next few minutes even?

The thought, though devastatingly appropriate,
was knocked suddenly out of his head. His hand
reached automatically for the gun at his hip.

The shots, a cluster of them it seemed, had come
from someplace up ahead but not far away,
certainly not far away.

It was awkward running in high-heeled riding boots, but that he did, keeping his hand on the butt of his gun – the warm feel of it and an urgency pushing him on.

He turned a corner and he remembered then where he was. A gambling house here. A gambling house that had always been here. As long as he could remember anyway.

This was one of the places he'd sought, would have certainly found his way to once he had his bearings right in this changing town.

He wasn't surprised to see the place still here. It belonged to this part of town, the back o' town, the nether world. Every Western township, even the more law-abiding ones, had its back o' town, and Lobo Forks had once had more than its fair share.

This gambling hall had always been one of the best of its kind in the territory. Quest had won and lost money here, had been in scrapes here.

Once he had almost had his left ear sliced off by a drunken loser over a poker table. He still bore the scar and when he looked at himself in the mirror at certain angles he thought the damaged ear looked kind of misshapen.

But the gink who had wielded the knife didn't do that at all well now, after Quest had broken the arm in two places and, without prompt treatment, it hadn't knitted well. The town hadn't had a proper doctor in those days.

The gambling house had batwings like any saloon. Quest kept himself low as he used his shoulder on them, twisting at the same time, a fast-moving and not very good target, if target he might become.

He hadn't paused to ask himself why he was butting in anyway; who did he think he was, Wyatt Earp in a foolish moment? Hell, anybody less foolish than Wyatt would be hard to find!

Quest himself had been a marshal once, hadn't he? He was purely acting like one now.

Maybe he had a reason. A premonition.

Seek and ye shall find.

Well, he'd certainly walked into this one.

Flat against the wall now beside the still-swinging batwings. His hand gripping the butt of the Smith and Wesson pistol but not pulling it yet. His eyes taking in with one sweeping glance the all-too-familiar scene before him: the huddle, the scatter, the staring, yammering faces.

Threatening movements?

Maybe.

He drew his gun.

5

He sensed a movement behind him and he whirled, gun lifted.

The shocked blue eyes of Crip looked up at him.

'It's only me, Obe.'

'I can see that, goddamit. Come round.'

He turned again and the small young man moved in front of him. Nobody it seemed was menacing anybody now.

'I heard shooting,' said Crip. 'What happened?'

There were a lot of answers, none of which made a lot of sense. Quest moved and Crip followed him now and they reached the centre of the room as the folks washed away each side of them.

There was a body on the sawdust-sprinkled floor and an upturned chair, a man with the front of his head blown away and the sawdust drying the blood in a brown mess.

'How'd this happen?' Quest asked, and there was authority in his voice.

The voices started up again. A clamour. Quest

pointed a finger at a big man who stood right in front of him.

'You tell me.'

'He was my pard.'

'You tell me!'

'It was a feller called hisself Beckon. A goddam card-sharp. Jeff – the man pointed a shaky finger at the corpse, – 'Jeff caught 'im at it an' braced him. Beckon shot him acrost the table. Jeff never had a chance.'

The voices started up again, backing what the big man had said.

Somebody else said, looking at Quest, 'Beckon ran out. You could've seen him.'

'I didn't see anybody.'

'Neither did I,' put in Crip.

'Tell it all, Cal,' said another voice, and the big man whose pard had been killed said, 'I took a shot at Beckon as he went through the doors. He staggered, so I must've hit 'im. But I don't know how bad.'

'I didn't hear any horse....'

'Nor me.' That was Crip again, and Quest gave him an irritable glance. The angel-faced button was beginning to get on his nerves.

'Mebbe you hit him worse than you think. Mebbe he's lying someplace.'

'Yeh, we'll go look.' The big man called Cal strode past the tall man and his diminutive companion. Others followed. But then Quest, not wasting any time, shouldered ahead of them, Crip following like the tail of a kite.

* * *

They searched, found nothing. The tall man whom most people now knew to be Obadiah Quest rode out of Lobo Forks on his high-stepping grey stallion.

There were some hard words but nobody followed the tall man on the grey horse. Not right then anyway. Somebody said that Septimus, the town constable, should be notified of the killing. Somebody else laughed. Obadiah Quest didn't even look back.

Crip had disappeared as if off on some secret business of his own. He hadn't followed Quest this time. He was no horseman anyway, everybody knew that. He was a small sneaking jackal and nobody followed *him*....

The giant Pecos George had left his store in order to stroll down to the doc's place to see how his erstwhile opponent young Jigger was getting on. He was contrite. But Jigger didn't blame him, said it was all in the game. The game that was finished for him now, though he didn't say so. Maybe the doc hadn't told him.

George joined the group on the edge of town and asked what was going on. He hadn't heard any shooting. He was told about the killing, the rest. He said, 'Leave it to Quest. He knows what to do.'

By this time the tall man with the thick red-gold hair was on the grey horse outside of town, had set his steed at a steady mile-eating trot, man and beast like an entity.

He hadn't seen anything moving ahead of him,
and now a range of low hills appeared on the
horizon.

They were clearer to his sight when he saw
movement and his horse snorted, for whether
friend or foe that was another horse there
browsing with head down but, as the newcomers
approached, warily stretching his long neck and
gazing at them.

Quest's horse whinnied, but the other beast, a
brown gelding, didn't reply, turning away. Then
Quest saw the still form on the ground and the
brown horse nosed at it but it still didn't move.

Quest dismounted, strode forward, went down
on one knee beside the still figure which lay curled
on its side, revealing the wound in the back, more
over to the left-hand side. Obviously a bullet
wound. A bad one.

The man was still alive but in a very bad way.

The brown was backing away. Quest called to
him gently and, though reluctantly at first, he
obeyed the deep reassuring voice and approached.

He was a mite skittish again as the tall man
lifted the body to the saddle while the man's own
mount looked on quizzically. But eventually it
was all done, Quest lashing the unconscious
man's arm around the brown horse's neck with
rawhide as comfortable as possible in case the
patient came to his senses, though that hardly
seemed likely.

Would he last back to town? Quest mounted up.
The grey waited for his rider's gentle pressure of

knee, the only signal needed. The brown was not
fractious now. The man took the brown's rein.

'Come on now, horse. C'mon now.'

Then they were moving. The journey back to
Lobo Forks took longer than when Quest and the
grey were outward bound. They were in sight of
the town when the posse came out to meet them,
at its head a lean, elderly man with pince-nez who
sat somewhat awkwardly in the saddle; and an
equally uncomfortable looking Crip on a small
Indian pony at his side.

Was angel-face sticking his neck out at last; or
did he have some ulterior motive?

The big man called Cal was there also of course.

'That's 'im,' Cal cried. 'That's 'im! That's Buck
Beckon.'

'Obe,' cried Crip, 'this 'ere is the town constable,
Mr Septimus Lagg.'

Septimus tweaked the brim of his hat and said,
'Glad to meet you, Mr Quest,' and the tall man
wondered if he meant that.

A courteous cuss anyway. 'Likewise,' replied
Quest.

'We ought to hang 'im,' cried big Cal, who
obviously had a one-track mind.

Septimus turned on him with a severe
expression and snapped, 'The law must take its
course.'

'What law?'

'Maybe he's dead already anyway,' said another
member of the seven-man posse. Quest had
counted them, wondering who'd be for him and

who agin him if the chips were down in some kind
of challenge.

He had taken a good look again at his
unconscious captive. 'He's still alive. But he won't
be if we stay here gabbin' too long.'

'He shot down my friend Jeff in cold blood,' said
big Cal self-righteously.

'The truth of that will have to be ascertained,'
said Septimus Lagg who was obviously a strict
advocate of law as it should be and not the rough
law of the frontier.

The elderly lawyer (or whatever he was, or
thought he was) concluded, 'We will take him to
the doctor.'

He turned his horse about and the others
followed. The man obviously had a bit of hold on
these people, Quest thought, as he with his
captive brought up the rear. He hadn't made up
his mind about friend Septimus, but he couldn't
say that he disliked the man, a confident gent, an
idealist, *whatever*.

'It'll be touch and go,' the rotund sawbones said.
'But there's a bullet in there and I'll have to get it
out anyway.'

'I'll stay with him,' said Obadiah Quest and the
others left, if reluctantly, particularly in the case
of big Cal and cadaverous Septimus.

At first Quest didn't notice that small Crip was
still hanging back, but, when he did, asked
harshly, 'What do you want?'

Crip pointed at the still form on the couch. He
said surprisingly, 'That man Beckon is my friend.

I want to know how he goes on.' He turned anxious blue eyes on the small, plump medico. 'Can I do anything, Doc?'

'You can go fetch Miss Della if you will.'

'Right.' Crip was swiftly gone.

It was Quest's turn to ask if he could do anything. The plump man turned irritably away from his patient and said, 'Not right now.'

'I'll go look in on young Jigger then, huh?'

'All right.'

But Jigger, in the adjoining room, was asleep, his battered face set. Quest shook his head slowly from side to side as he turned away. Leaving the room, he almost ran into a young woman. She and Crip had come silently up the stairs. Crip always moved like a small ghost.

And this girl wore Indian moccasins.

That, however, was the only Indian thing about her.

6

Her hair was the colour of corn, long and curly and kind of wind-blown. The eyes that looked at Quest were of a bright bluey-grey and bold, almost challenging.

They enlivened a smooth, pretty, golden-tanned face and the man could tell from the way she moved that she had a pretty body also. Then she was past him, Crip at her heels, and into the room where Beckon lay and the doc waited. And Quest heard him say: 'Hallo, Della.'

'Hallo, Doc Keane. You need me, huh?'

'Looks like it.'

Then Quest was in the room which wasn't too large and suddenly seemed crammed with people.

'I don't need you two anymore,' snapped the doc. 'Come back later if you wish, though I'm not promising what your friend will be like if you do.'

Crip and Quest took their leave and Quest decided that he wasn't mad at the little feller any more.

Then Crip said, 'He was the one you came here

after, wasn't he? Beckon? Buck Beckon?'

'How did you know?'

'He told me.'

'And he asked you to keep an eye on me, huh?'

'Somep'n like that.' Crip was almost aggressive now and that wasn't like him at all.

'What else did he tell you?'

'Nothing.'

'Like why I was after him for instance?'

'Nothing, I said.' Crip was petulant now.

'I arranged to meet Elias Slack in the Dirty Ace,' said Quest.

'Mind if I come along?'

'Suit yourself.'

Elias was waiting. The saloon was strangely quiet. Darkness was falling; lamps were lit, a welcoming sight.

Elias said that many folks were down at the Golden Palace. Quest was reminded that the Golden Palace was – and always had been – the name of the gambling hall where Buck Beckon had shot to death the feller called Jeff who'd been a friend to big Cal.

'I'll go take a look,' said Crip.

'Watch your ass,' said Elias.

The batwings swung behind the little man and Elias went on, 'He aims to get to know everythin' that goes on, and sometimes he knows a lot.'

Quest had no comment on that. 'That big Cal,' said Elias, 'he's a troublemaker, an' if he's at the Golden Palace – and I figure he is – a mob could be gathering an' they'll want young Buck's scalp.'

'Could be.'

'Buck ain't in no fit state to fight 'em.'

'He ain't in no fit state at all,' said Quest.

'Anybody with the doc?'

'When I left just a purty gel called Della.'

'She's a prime one, Della. A young widder-woman....'

'I didn't figure ...'

'Her man got hisself killed about a twelve-month ago. Got in a fight here, right in the middle o' this floor. Got his head broken, never came out of it. He'd worked at one o' the ranches outside town and had just got hisself canned for fighting. He was insanely jealous of Della, for no firm reason far's I know, though there'd allus been others after her.'

'That figures.'

'Yeh. Well, Della worked at the ranch too, sort of housekeeper, and one of the other cowboys looked sideways at her and Billy – that was Della's man – knocked two of his teeth out. And it wasn't the first time Billy had taken umbrage, and the boss had warned him.

'Well, Billy came back here an' two barflies started to chivvy him and a fight started and Billy got his come-uppance. He wasn't a big feller when he was straight. Sort of an accident y'know, nobody could be actually blamed.'

'No.'

'Della left the ranch, and works now with a friend of hers who runs a millinery shop. She helps out the doc sometimes, had plenty of

practice patching up Billy in the past I guess.
Luckily they had no kids.'

'She attached again now?'

'Not far as I know.'

Crip came back in, dancing like he had ants in
his pants, said, 'There's a mob from the Golden
Palace an' it's moving, big Cal leading 'em.'

'Come on,' said Quest and he moved.

Elias hadn't needed any signal, Quest knew
that, knew the hunch-shouldered man was at his
heels. But Crip now would be well in the
background, or maybe gone: he was no fighter.

But Elias it seemed soon had an idea for Crip,
whirled on him.

'Go get as many of my boys as you can find, fast.'

'All right.'

Then, with Crip already disappeared, Elias
danced in front of Quest. Despite his shoulder
disability the old prizefighter was still quick on
his feet. He jabbed a finger. 'Through this alley,
Obe, an' round the backs. We could get to the doc's
place before that cattle.'

A network of back-doubles. And from time to
time they could hear the ominous murmurings of
the mob and now and then a shout.

The two men reached their destination and
Elias tried the back door, said, 'It's locked.'

The clamourings of the mob in the street out
front were clearer now.

Elias carried a gun low on his hip. It was an old
but well-kept Colt Dragoon, a formidable weapon.
He took it from its holster and used its long barrel

to hammer on the door while both he and Quest
yelled for Doc or whoever else indoors who could
listen.

'Hark,' said Quest, and then they were both
quiet, hearing footsteps on boards.

'Who is it?' It was the girl's voice.

'It's Elias Slack and Obadiah Quest. Open the
door, Della, we want to help.'

A bolt was drawn, a key turned. The golden-
haired girl stepped aside to let them through.
Now they heard the crowd noises more clearly and
they seemed right outside. A thin voice yelled,
'Open up, Doc.'

A louder one threatened, 'We'll break it down.'

Della locked and bolted the door behind her.
Elias said, 'Young Crip will be bringing some of
my people. Will you listen for them, honey?'

'I will, Mr Slack.' She lingered behind.

With the doc now was his friend, lean, elderly
Septimus Lagg who, as town constable, you might
have thought was entitled to be present. He
looked stern but not scared. The doc looked
fiercely indignant and had an old horse pistol in
his plump fist.

He turned towards the two newcomers and
Elias Slack said, 'Leave this to the professionals.'
And Septimus Lagg said, 'He's right, Noah.'

He obviously had no weapon himself. Somebody
was banging on the front door. 'I'm going out to
them,' Septimus added and he moved.

Obadiah Quest said, 'Stay where you are, Mr
Lagg.'

'Yeh,' said Elias. 'If anybody's goin' out there it's Obe an' me.'

There was a yell from the neighbouring room. 'What's goin' on?' Young Jigger was awake. But, on the bed behind the doctor and Septimus, Buck Beckon was still and silent, breathing only gently, eyes closed, face like death.

There was more yelling from outside, more banging, the noise resounding through the house. Over it though, Jigger's voice sounded louder now. Doc left the room and soon Jigger was quiet but the noise from outside didn't abate.

Doc came back, said, 'I've quietened the boy down. He shouldn't be disturbing himself, he should be resting.'

The plump medico had put his horse pistol on the bedside table. Elias still had his Dragoon in his fist. Quest had unholstered his side-arm, his Smith and Wesson. In the back of his belt too, in a smaller, purposely made pouch he had a Bulldog pistol and, next to that, in another pouch made of bearskin, a knife which wasn't as big as a bowie but quite as formidable.

'I'll get out there before they break the door down,' he said as more blows resounded through the house. He moved. Elias moved.

Quest turned his head. 'You don't....'

'I reckon I have a bigger stake in this town than you have,' said Elias tartly and he kept moving. He and his tall friend were almost abreast when they reached the door of the room but then Elias gave a small concession, politely let Obe go first.

'Mebbe they're just funnin',' the ex-pugilist said.

'Like hell,' said Quest, as ahead of them there was a grim splintering sound.

But then noise came from behind them and Septimus called, 'We've got some more help.'

It was some of Elias's people – most of them in fact. And, surprisingly, Crip was still with them.

'Follow us, boys,' said Elias, and his boys did, all seven of them.

Now Crip stayed behind, looking down at the still form of his friend Buck Beckon.

7

Della called, 'I'll keep watch out back.'

'One of you go with her,' said Elias. 'You, Johnny.'

A determined-looking youngster with blond hair that almost matched the girl's, though it was very much shorter, detached himself from the rest and followed Della, doubtless admiring the pretty way she moved.

The others went on out in the other direction, Quest still in the lead, Elias close behind him.

They reached the hall as the front door crashed open, a prime attack now if ever there was one. Big Cal bulled in and he had a gun in his hand. His eyes started when he came face to face with Quest.

The tall man lashed out with his weapon and the barrel slashed across Cal's face. It was a cruel blow, fetching blood immediately, and the man who'd received it dropped his own gun and staggered back into the people behind him.

Perforce, they had to back down the steps, and

now the defending force followed them, warriors
adept with their fists and some of them with more
lethal weapons also.

One of Elias's boys dragged the unconscious
form of Cal down the steps and dumped him on
the boardwalk below as the crowd backed. They
outnumbered the defenders by two to one but they
didn't look so belligerent now, their leader like a
red doll at their feet.

As usual a few pressed from the back and
yelled. They were, comparatively, out of harm's
way. But those at the front weren't so lucky and
two men were jostled into a pair of Elias's boys
and suffered accordingly, one with a broken nose,
the other with a mouth that looked as if a mule
had kicked it, causing a painful loss of blood and a
few teeth.

Most of the defenders, pugilists all, had guns in
their fists now, aping their leader Elias and his
friend Obe. The latter stood tall on the stoop and
raised his voice.

'Go on about your normal business, folks, before
somebody else gets hurt; and hurt mightily
maybe.'

Some began to drift away, for that had been a
reasonable request after all, if somewhat
menacing. And Obadiah Quest had the rep to back
it up.

'Take him with you,' said Quest and he was
snarling now as he indicated the fallen Cal who
had begun to moan like a big sick cow.

That broke up the folk at the front of the crowd

as two of them came forward and collected their
erstwhile leader and toted him away.

There were a few more shouts flung back, a few
threatening gestures. But the only guns in sight
now were those in the hands of the men on the
steps and the stoop at the doc's place.

'Two of you boys stay an' watch 'em,' Elias said.

The rest went back inside. Jigger had begun to
call out again.

''Ark at him,' said Elias. 'You wouldn't think he'd
keep up his caterwauling. And him with a broken
jaw an' all.'

'I guess he's just inquisitive,' said Quest.

Della came out. What a picture she made,
thought Quest.

'Mr Beckon has opened his eyes,' she said.

Then they were all in the room again. The man
who'd been out in the yard with the girl said, 'It's
quiet out there.'

'Better hold there a while anyway,' said Elias.
'Just you, Johnny, if you don't mind.'

'I don't mind.' The man returned to his post.

'Obe.' The voice seemed to come from far away. It
was like the voice of a boy, a voice that was
beginning to break but wasn't all the way there yet.

The tall man moved towards the cot and the
voice spoke again and this time it was a mite
stronger. 'I want to talk to Obe. Just me an' Obe.'

They all looked at Doc Noah Keane who pursed
his lips as there was a small silence. Then the
plump medico said, 'All right. But not too long. It'd
be stupid to take chances now.'

The tall man with the thick red-gold hair crossed to the cot, sat on the chair beside it. The others left the room.

There was a bit of an altercation in the passage. Pecos George had turned up. He'd been down the other end of town, had hastened to the scene at the doc's office, hoping to be able to help, was peeved that he was a mite too late. He went in to Jigger. Things were pretty quiet again all round. But not too much time had elapsed when Doc went back to Quest and Beckon and broke up the discussion.

Beckon was left alone. In the passage, Doc said, 'He doesn't look too good. I'm still mighty worried about him.'

'I'm not too content myself,' said Quest. A funny way of putting it maybe, causing the doc to add tentatively, 'You and him were close, huh?'

'Sort of.'

At Elias's orders his boys were going about their business again, even the one being fetched in from out back, joining the others as they trooped from the house. They'd been told by their chief to keep an eye on the Dirty Ace and the Golden Palace. The town seemed quiet now, but even that could be an ominous sign instead of a welcome one.

Pecos George took his leave also, said young Jigger was mending well. Doc and Quest joined Della, Elias, and the omnipresent Crip, who was still hanging on.

As the two men entered the room Elias and Crip seemed to be arguing.

'He ain't exactly Obe's brother.' That was Elias talking.

'He's some kin anyway.' That was Crip.

Quest cut in on both of them. 'He's my cousin. But he lived with me an' my folks for many years and I guess we were kind of like brothers.'

The tall man didn't sound mad, just sort of tired, resigned, momentarily not like himself at all as his friends knew him, as others might have figured him.

'You were after him,' said Crip, as he had once said before to Quest.

Elias had known this also and now said, 'When he saw you, Obe, at the fight – you an' Pecos George – he ran. And you after him like a bat outa hell but came to grief.'

'I have the scars to prove that,' said Quest with a humourless smile.

'I can't figure then why he lit down at the Golden Palace afterwards, knowing you'd be bound to find him there sooner or later. And get in a card game to boot an' shoot a man an' get shot himself.'

'He didn't plan that part of it,' said Quest wryly. 'But, as for the other part, he had a change of heart – that's what he called it. He said he was all through running.'

The inevitable question had to be asked and it was Crip who asked it. 'Why was he running in the first place?'

Quest's eyes bored into the little man. 'Didn't he tell you that?'

'You know he didn't.' Crip was getting peevish again.

Quest didn't answer right away, went off at a tangent in fact, asking, 'Where's Septimus Lagg?' as if he'd only just noticed the elderly lawyer's absence.

'He's gone back to his office,' said Elias. 'He said he'd like to see you later, Obe.'

Crip, whose feet didn't quite touch the floor as he sat on his chair, was managing to drum his toes on the floor in his impatience. Elias, having answered Obe's question, was reflecting how damn' irritating that close-mouthed character could be when he set his mind to it.

Maybe Obe thought he'd said enough for the time being. But Elias himself was intrigued and impatient now himself. And Della and old Doc were leaning forward in their chairs.

'Buck always had guts,' Quest said. 'He ain't the running sort, but he's a chancer. He's quick with his hands, but he's never been too quick with a gun....'

'He was quick back in the Golden Palace I was told,' put in Crip.

'He was quicker than the man who faced him,' said Quest.

'That was Jeff an' he said Buck was cheating. So did Jeff's pard, big Cal.'

'I thought Buck Beckon was your friend.'

'He asked me to keep an eye out for you is all, let him know if you happened along. He figured you would eventually. An' you did. But when you first

turned up Buck was at the fights, layin' bets.
When he saw you I guess he lost his nerve for a
bit. But he got it back, didn't he?'

'I guess he did. And he was as cunning as he's
always been. He knew I wouldn't force a stand-up
fight with him in a crowded place like the Golden
Palace.

'I hope he's gonna be all right,' said the
mercurial Crip, his angel face taking on a
ludicrously anxious expression.

'I've done my best,' said Doc Keane. 'It's in the
lap of the gods now as they say.'

There was a lull in the conversation. Everybody
seemed to be waiting for Quest to speak again.
And he was taking his time.

There was quiet.

Then with explosive suddenness the silence was
broken.

No voices. But the twang of a rifle shot and the
sound of broken glass falling in another room.

A yell. It seemed to be coming from Jigger's
room. And more shots.

Quest was very quick, springing to his feet, his
eyes on Della first.

'Stay put, y'hear?'

She nodded, her blue eyes wide. Everybody else
was on their feet then; they followed Quest to the
door, Crip bringing up the rear. Della rose to her
feet but didn't follow the rest.

Jigger was sitting up in bed. His bandaged face
made him look like a clown. But a clown as mad as
a mother hen in a thunderstorm.

The window behind and to the right of him was shattered, slivers of glass on the floor beneath it. It looked out on the back of the house.

'Keep away from that window,' said Quest.

The warning was timely – as more whiplash reports sounded and the last shattered fragments of glass were precipitated from the window and its frame was chipped and scored.

'Jesus,' ejaculated Elias as a bullet zipped past his ear, thunked into the door behind him. But nobody was hit.

They crouched. Quest gave signals that were quickly picked up. Doc sat on the bed beside Jigger. Crip flattened himself against the wall.

Quest and Elias moved to positions at each side of the window and they both had their guns out.

There had been curtains but they were damaged, blowing in the breeze from the gap that had once been a pretty workmanlike window.

Both Obe and his friend Elias did some peeping. Like inquisitive old maids who aimed to find out why the neighbours were making such a racket.

'I can't see a thing,' said Elias.

'Me neither.'

8

'What's that?' said Elias.

'Hold it! The man's waving.'

'It's Pecos George. He doesn't seem armed.'

'What the hell...?'

Behind the big baldheaded bruiser were two privies side by side, like large upended coffins; a gap between them.

George turned about and went back to the privies and bent and reached into the gap.

He dragged forth a helpless figure, another man undoubtedly, but one obviously not nearly so healthy as George himself. He was dumped on the littered ground and George retreated, and turned again, in his hands a rifle which he waved aloft. Quest and Elias showed themselves to him then.

George marched forward at a stoop, dragging his unconscious captive – or maybe the man was dead – with one hand, sloping the rifle in the other.

The folks made for the back. In the passage they ran into Della.

'Nothing to worry about now, honey,' said Quest. 'Come with us.'

'All right, Mister Quest,' said the golden-haired girl, a snap in her voice but a roguish and not unfriendly look in her fine eyes.

The back door was locked and bolted but that barrier was soon overcome and Pecos George lugged his burden into the kitchen.

'Randy Digo,' said Crip. 'A friend of big Cal's. Was a friend of Jeff's.'

The man's swarthy face looked as if it had been rammed forcibly into a brick wall.

'He's still alive,' said Pecos George. 'I was out back dumping some rubbish when I heard the shots an' spotted him. I moved up quietly behind him an' he turned on me an' I hit him smack in the jib.'

'One o' your specialities,' said Elias 'Mad Boy' Slack admiringly. Randy Digo looked as if he was going to sleep for a week.

'Hell, he was drunk,' said big George. 'He was a shootin' fool.'

'Whether or not,' said Crip, 'Randy was always good with a rifle.'

'Randy allus was an idiot as well,' said George as he placed the long Winchester on the kitchen table. It looked like a fine gun.

Crip said, 'He was in that mob earlier was Randy. He was just trying to get his own back I guess, him and his booze an' his favourite long gun.'

'Mebbe he was grievin' for his friend Jeff,' said

Big George caustically.

All faces were turned in the direction of the communicating door and the sound of approaching footsteps.

Septimus Lagg appeared, came to a stop, said haltingly, 'I was coming back here when I heard the shots.'

'No harm to anybody,' said Obadiah Quest. ''Cept to him.' The tall man jerked a thumb in the direction of the prone man on the floor.

Doc Keane was looking at his old friend and now said, 'Jesus, old son, you look ill.'

'I felt rocky when I got up this morning, Noah,' said the lean oldster. 'Seemed like food poisoning or something like that....'

'I'm the doctor,' said Keane caustically. 'You ask me.'

'I was going to. And then all that happened. It was maybe some salt pork I had last night.'

'And what's wrong with good honest beef?'

'Nothing.... I had to leave earlier, clear my gut, lay down. But then this shooting started and I guess it sort of revitalized me.' Septimus smiled wryly, but his bony forehead was bedewed with sweat.

'Go an' sit in that comfortable armchair in my little office. I'll come see you in a bit.'

'I'll be all right.' But the lawyer took his leave.

Randy Digo was beginning to moan and stir.

'I'll have to fix that face I guess,' said Doc. 'Though I have to say that old Septimus, though he hasn't been whacked or shot, is a more deserving case.' He bent over the twitching form. 'Help me to get him up, put him on that trestle in the hall. Pretty soon I'm going to run out o' lying-down space if this town mayhem continues.'

As Randy was carried into the hall, be became a mite more vociferous. Doc continued with his wry comments. 'Come to think of it, Cal hasn't been back to have his face fixed.'

'He won't,' said Elias Slack. 'He'd be wondering what would next meet him here if he showed that face again. He'll go to old Injun Perce I guess.'

'The old half-breed who used to be swamper at the Dirty Ace?' said Obadiah Quest. 'Is he still alive?'

'He is. And he's still the swamper at the saloon, and doing his medicine-man act at that. I'm told he ain't half bad.'

'One o' these days that old faker's going to kill somebody,' said the present medico darkly.

'Maybe he'll kill big Cal,' said Elias and everybody laughed, but not too much.

Randy Digo was swearing, blood dripping from his chin as he struggled. The doctor bent over him and said, 'Keep still, you jackass. And mind your language.'

Somebody else was calling out. Della withdrew.

She came back, said, 'Mr Quest, Septimus Lagg would like to see you if you can spare the time.'

He grinned at her challenging tartness, said nothing, went down the hall to the study.

The elderly town constable-cum-lawyer was half-sitting half-reclining in the big cushion-piled

armchair behind the desk. He looked a bit
brighter, gesturing with a lean hand. 'I have a
proposition to put to you, Mr Quest.'

Quest sat down on the wooden chair on his side
of the desk.

Later Quest and his old sparring partner Elias
walked down the street together.

The latter said, 'Lobo Forks hasn't ever had a
jailhouse, not as far as I remember anyway.'

'No, I don't remember one either.'

'But I'll show you the place Septimus mentioned
to you. I guess Randy Digo will have to be put
there when the doc's fixed him up. And mebbe big
Cal too.'

'We'll see.'

'You'll need some help.'

'I'll manage.'

'Hell, I ain't leavin' in the middle o' the night.
Me nor my boys.'

But Quest had nothing to say to this, went off at
a tangent in fact. 'Kind of a coincidence happened.
Or is going to happen.'

'What's that?'

'Remember our old friend Judge Cracker?'

'Sure do.'

'He's also a friend of Septimus Lagg, though I
didn't know that. Old colleagues when they first
started out lawyering it seems. The judge is
coming to visit Septimus in a coupla days.
Septimus wants the judge to stand up for me,
swear me in, him bein' a judge an' all 'stead o' just

a lawyer. He's a retired judge actually – but what
the hell! Septimus seem to think things will be
more legal that way.'

'He's a stickler for legalities Septimus is,' said
Elias. 'So you're goin' through with this all
shipshape then?'

'Yeh. I told Septimus he doesn't need a
gunfighter, the town doesn't. And that's what I
am, a gunfighter. And one gunfighter brings
others who think they're tougher an' faster than
he is, who want to make a quick rep for
themselves.'

'Yeh.'

'But Septimus said this has been an outlaw
town anyway....'

'I know what he means. But gunfighter or not,
fast rep or not, you've been badged before. And the
town's changing now and purely needs a
marshal.... And you've got connections here now,
what with Buck an' all, and him sick,' Elias added
haltingly.

'Yeh, there is that of course,' said Quest. 'I
guess I ought to tell you the rest of that now.
About me an' Buck an' the old man.'

'I was sorry to hear about the old man. And you
opined that Buck was responsible for his death.'

9

'We'll go someplace quiet and I'll tell you the whole story,' Quest said, 'and Buck's side of it.'

'Do you believe Buck's side of it?'

'I dunno. Even as a kid Buck was a storyteller. And he turned out later to be a sort of confidence man as well as a gambler.'

'And a cardsharp the way Jeff told it.'

'But Jeff ain't here to tell it now, is he? He's in the funeral parlour.'

'Big Cal ain't, an' he's telling it loud. And I'll tell you somep'n else now, pardner. Big Cal will be on the prod after you, marshal or no marshal.'

'Yeh, I've got to expect that I guess.'

'Don't sell that man short, Obe. Cal had a rep in the Pecos territory I'm told. Killed men up there before he came here, mebbe on the run.'

'Mebbe I can arrest him then,' said Quest sardonically.

Elias laughed shortly, pointed. 'There it is. That's what you wanted to see first, ain't it?'

'I guess.'

It was an adobe foursquare building of one
storey. It was near the edge of town and debris
blown by the wind was clustered against it. It had
a door in the centre as the two men faced it, and a
window at each side, both of them glassed but
only jagged shards of this remaining, glinting
redly in the dying sun.

Elias said, 'There's a back door,' and led the way
round the side of the building. 'I guess maybe we
should've waited an' then brought that rifle-toting
half-breed with us after Doc had patched his face.
We could've put him in here an' tried him for size,
sort of.'

Quest laughed. 'And have him crawl through
the window? Anyway Pecos George said he'd stay
with Doc a while, and Septimus is still there
resting up.'

There was more rubbish. The back door was
intact but had no lock and the two men opened it
and walked through.

'God, it stinks in here,' said Quest.

Elias said, 'A crazy old prospector lived here off
and on. He ain't been back for nigh on a
twelve-month though, and everybody figures he's
dead. 'Less he's made his fortune at last and is
living in luxury in Chicago or Kansas City.'

There were two biggish rooms and a tiny
kitchen. 'It could be converted easily and the
doors and window fixed,' said Elias. 'Locks an'
bars y'know.'

'I guess.'

There wasn't much furniture, and grass, tree

debris and tumbleweeds had come through the windows and festooned the shadowy interior like ghostly trailing vines and rotting moss. There was a pervading odour of damp.

'Nobody could live here,' said Quest. 'Not yet anyway.'

Elias chuckled. 'You'll have to live someplace else then till the place is fixed. I reckon I've got a spare pup tent. What do you think of the place anyway?'

'It'll do.'

'It'll soon get fixed. There'll be plenty o' volunteers. This town is changing.' Elias chuckled again. 'Sure thing. And more to come. A new marshal. And a jailhouse to boot.'

But Obe had gone all enigmatic again, just made for the front door, walking purposefully, skirting the debris neatly, a man whose movements were economical and graceful.

He found the front door locked, bolted on the inside which was kind of strange with the back door being easily accessible. But soon they were out in the fresh air again and were both impelled to take great gulps of it.

They walked again and they didn't talk much. They ranged the town. Elias Slack had a lot of friends here. They got promises of materials and labour from various folk, the work to be started tomorrow morning. It was getting near dusk.

The two friends had learned a few things. They'd learned that big Cal, doctored by swamper and would-be medicine man old Injun Perce was

lying in his room above the Dirty Ace and vowing
to get Obadiah Quest. As soon as he could move
around and see straight.

'I guess you owe him for Buck anyway,' Elias
said to Obe. 'Although Buck shot Cal's friend Jeff
and we don't rightly know who was to blame, Cal
did shoot Buck in the back. But do you want to get
Cal for that – or do you want to get Buck an' Cal
both when they both get fit? I ask you.'

'I ain't sure that Buck will ever be quite right'
again,' said Quest.

Feeling that, after reflection, it wouldn't be too
politic to go to the Dirty Ace right then, they went
instead to the Golden Palace. Although this was
mainly a gambling establishment it sold good food
and booze as well and some of that mixture was
what both men needed.

They chose a table in a corner away from the
gaming layouts and Elias made a sign to a fat
Mexican girl who greeted him like an old friend.
She took their orders for both the food and the
drinks and she wobbled away not too
ungracefully.

Watching her Elias said, 'When I first knew her
she was as slim as a doe, and as pretty. We had a
thing going for a while – every time I visited Lobo
Forks anyway. But then she got married an' had a
coupla kids. Her husband got stabbed to death in
a fight right here in this place. They were on the
outs then anyway, so I heard afterwards. Now she
and the kids live upstairs with Carlo. He's got
plenty o' room.'

Quest remembered Carlo as being proprietor of the Golden Palace but didn't know him well.

The food arrived. They had well-baked fritters of chopped beef, potatoes and onions flavoured with spices and beans and cabbage and tomatoes on the side, followed by plum and apple pie and lashings of coffee.

The Mexican woman, who was called Jeanna, then brought them a small bottle of brandy and two glasses and told them that this was with the compliments of the management.

'Where is Carlo?' Elias asked.

'He's in bed with the croup. I told him you were here but he couldn't come down.'

'Give him our compliments an' tell him to get well soon.'

'I will.' Jeanna swayed away again.

The two men lit cheroots, a small packet of which lay on the tray with the brandy. They poured some brandy, tasted it.

'Good stuff,' said Quest.

'Yeh. And Carlo could be an ally y'know.'

'It pays the gambling fraternity to play along with the local law,' said Quest. 'If they've got any sense that is.'

'Carlo's got sense,' Elias said.

They sipped. They smoked. They looked at each other.

Quest said, 'Lots of folks thought Buck was my brother. Despite the different names, that is.'

'Folks could do that. Names don't mean a lot in the West. Folks choose themselves a new name if they don't like the one they've got. Or for other reasons o' course.'

'Buck ain't even my half-brother, you know that now. He's my cousin. My father took him in as a tad when his folks died. He was an only son. Dad treated him like a son too, and for quite a time we were like brothers. But as Buck grew he changed....'

'He was allus on the lookout for the main chance.'

'Right! He gambled, he lied, he cheated; and he was always into Dad for money and with the spread to run – small though it was – the old man couldn't always stand it. Me an' Buck had some stand-up fights about that. He used to go away, used to come back. We never knew where he'd been, what he'd done. He was away when I went away too, couldn't stand ranch life, joined up with you and your lot.'

'And went on from there,' said Elias.

'That's it. I visited the old man from time to time. Buck had been and gone. I only ran into him a coupla times. He never became a real gunny I guess, but he was pretty well everything else....'

'He couldn't ever match you with a gun.'

'The old man was getting long in the tooth, and he wasn't too well. When he died I was someplace else, I heard it from somebody else. I went back right away....'

'You would do o' course.'

'I heard it from a neighbour. Buck had been there desperate for money, had threatened the old

man, so the neighbour said, though to be fair I
didn't know the rights of that.'

'No.'

'The old man was sick, had only just left his bed.
He hitched up the gig an' the little trotter and he
went into town to the bank to try an' get a loan,
some money for Buck. Coming back he fell off his
seat – a sort of seizure the doc said. He held on to
the reins and was dragged till the horse stopped.
The doc said the old man must've been dead by
then.'

'So that's what you meant when you said Buck
was responsible for your father's death?'

'Well, he was, wasn't he?'

'I guess.'

'Buck stayed for the funeral. When I got there
just afterwards he'd gone. And he'd taken his
blood money with him.'

'Well, I see – it figures. So now you want it out of
him?'

'Mebbe he's got his come-uppance already,' said
Quest. Then he was silent.

Elias rose slowly to his feet. 'Let's go back to the
doc's place an' see how things are getting on,' he
said.

10

As they walked Obe began to talk again,
surprising Elias.

'Buck couldn't talk much. But he did his best I
guess. Banged up like he was I guess he did pretty
good by his lights. He allus was a good storyteller.'

'You said that before.'

'I know. I'm kinda repeating myself, trying to
get things right in my mind....'

'That's understandable. You and Buck were
mighty close once.'

'He said he didn't aim for the old man to go to
the bank. He said that the old man volunteered,
insisted. He said he was leaving, figuring that if
the old man got the money he could use it himself
for the ranch. He said he was gonna write a note....
Then two neighbours brought the old man in the
way they'd found him out on the trail. He said he'd
taken the money 'cos he figured the old man would
want him to have it, and I wasn't around anyway.'

'And that's eating at you now, huh?'

'Could be.'

They entered Doc Keane's place.

Randy Digo sat on the trestle in the hall, holding his bandaged head in his hands. He had, of course, been relieved of all his hardware. He didn't even look up as they entered. He didn't look as if he were about to go any place yet whether under his own steam or anybody else's.

Both Jigger and Buck were sleeping. Jigger looked fine, was breathing like a contented infant, an infant who'd recently banged his cranium into a wall.

'Hell of a lot of damaged jibs around lately,' Elias Slack commented. 'Digo, Jigger. Even you, bucko. You still bear marks were Pecos George tattooed you.'

'I tattooed him back.'

'You surely did, bucko. You surely did.'

Pecos George had gone back to his store. Delectable Della had taken her leave also.

Doc and his friend Septimus were sitting in the study talking. Septimus looked a whole lot better than he had earlier.

Doc's verdict on Buck Beckon's condition was an ambiguous one.

He had some other news for Obadiah Quest though.

'Della told me to tell you that she and her friend Polly have a spare room at their place if you want temporary accommodation till you get fixed up properly.'

'That sounds fine.'

'I showed you the shop,' said Elias.

'Yeh. I'll go down there a mite later.'

He didn't wait long though: he was impelled to see the delectable Della again. *Delectable!* Judge Cracker would love that word. Quest would be seeing the old judge again pretty soon.

He went into the hall and Randy Digo came up from his trestle with fists swinging, one eye glaring fearsomely over the white bandages.

The man was as wild as a mustang with burning mesquite under his tail. One of the fists caught Quest with a glancing blow on a cheekbone, a place already bruised during the fight with Pecos George. Quest staggered.

Randy's second swing missed entirely and his fist slammed into the door jamb behind its intended target. Then the other man regained his equilibrium and punched Randy square in his middle, bending him up with a great gulp, knocking all the wind from him.

Randy was manhandled back on to his improvised resting place.

Septimus and Doc came out to see what the commotion was about.

Quest said, 'I want some rope.'

He lashed Randy hand and foot with rope supplied by Elias, who now also put in an appearance – he'd been to the privy out back.

'I guess that should've been done beforehand,' said the elderly fight promoter.

There were no more comments on this. The door slammed – and there was small Crip; and Elias, who obviously had no great liking for that particular blue-eyed boy, turned on him.

'Where've you been?'

'Out!' Crip seemed to be getting uppity. 'What happened?' he asked.

'This character attacked Obe.'

Crip seemed to think this was funny. 'Didn't do 'im much good, did it?'

'Wouldn't have happened mebbe if you'd stayed here, watching.'

'I had to go out. I have a restless disposition.'

'So has a coyote.'

'That's a pretty wounding sort of thing to say, Elias.'

'All right, I'll take it back. Mebbe I should've said chipmunk.'

Randy had his breath back and began to swear.

'You shut your mouth or I'll gag you,' said Quest.

Randy shut up. Doc Keane said, 'Turn him on his side in case he wants to be sick.'

Crip began to chuckle. 'Help me, jackass,' said Elias.

Randy was made more comfortable. There wasn't much room for him to curl up, but he did his best.

'I'm goin' down the street a piece,' said Quest and he left.

The night was dark and there were lights both sides of him as he walked, the heels of his riding boots going *clack-clack* on the muddy, brittle wood of the boardwalk which was broken in places, creating treacherous gaps. And in some places there wasn't any boardwalk at all and the narrow spiderlike tributaries which ran off the main street like trickles from a muddy river were holed and uneven and very dark where no light penetrated.

Quest had his wits about him, and his roving eyes. If he became marshal of this town he would do this walk at odd times every night: it was on the cards. He'd sweep the alleys, and his gunhand would be itchy.

He wasn't a marshal yet. He was a private man. But he was already a target, as Randy Digo had recently proved to him. An idiotic drunk.

But there were others who wouldn't be idiotic or drunk. The wolves would gather....

But he had a stake in this town now.

The millinery shop had finished business for the day but there was a light in the back of it coming from a door that was ajar. The front door was locked and he didn't blame the girls for that. He rapped with his fist on the glass panel above the wood and heard the sound ringing inside.

There were quick footsteps as the inner door swung open, spilling more light against which the figure of the girl was limned. He recognized that beautiful shape. It was statuesque as it halted, but it was also very womanly and seductive.

Her voice called, 'Who is that?'

'It's me, Obe Quest.'

She unlocked the door and opened it. For a moment as she closed it behind him, locking it again, they were very close to each other.

She smelled fresh, but it was a woman smell, an elusive thing that stirred him. Then she was moving away from him, leading the way, swaying lightly in moccasins, her variant of lounging slippers no doubt. She flung over her shoulder, 'You haven't met Polly, have you?'

'Nope.'

'She's my partner. Also my best friend.'

Then they were into the brighter light and a redheaded plump, homely faced girl rose to meet the newcomer.

'Polly, this is Obadiah Quest I told you about, Lobo Forks' first marshal.'

'It ain't certain sure yet,' said the tall man as he took Polly's small hand in his own.

Her grip was warm. There was a shyness about her. She was no raving beauty but had kind, trustful brown eyes and a good smile and her abundant red hair was her crowning glory.

'Miss Polly.'

'Mr Quest. Will you take coffee, suh?'

'I'm obliged to you.'

'Sit down, Obe,' said Della as if she'd known him all her life.

She was the bold one, and he reacted to this. 'Thank you kindly, honey.'

Sitting on an old armchair which suited him well, he felt Polly's gaze directly on him; it passed quickly to her friend before the redheaded girl withdrew, soon returning with coffee on a tray and cookies she had baked herself. These were delicious. After his big meal at the Golden Palace he was far from hungry, but he wolfed three cookies and told Polly how good they were.

'She's the champion cook out of both of us,' Della said.

11

A door was rapped. This time it was the back door.

'I'll get it,' Polly said.

When she returned she had a young man with her. Dark, handsome. Well-britched Quest might have said. But he reserved judgement. A feller younger than himself, with an arrogant way with him and a low-slung gun in a fancy rig.

Quest stood up though, and Polly introduced him to Derry Saxe, describing him as her 'friend'. Derry said 'Mr Quest' and tested his grip on the tall man, eyeing him with no great friendliness.

Derry soon made himself at home, lounging in his chair with his legs stretched out in front of him. He was a mite shorter than Quest. He took coffee. He didn't ask the girls for permission to smoke but took out a packet of long, thin cheroots, extracted one, lit up.

As if on an afterthought he offered Quest one. The latter said he'd stick to his 'makings' – if the ladies didn't object.

They didn't. He took out his baccy and his

papers. The two girls watched him. Derry, wreathed in smoke, feigned indifference.

Quest lit up. There was no actual constraint now, but talk was desultory. Derry said his 'ceegar' was good. Quest said the latest tobacco in his small hide pouch came from El Paso. Derry said he'd never been to El Paso.

Finishing his cigarette, Quest decided to take his leave. The girls told him he must call again and their bright faces had warmth.

'So long, marshal,' said Derry.

Now why did that jasper call me 'marshal', Quest thought, as Della let him out through the front door and they gripped hands before she closed the door behind him and he heard her lock and bolt it.

Maybe they should've done more than just clasp hands, that was another thought.

Quest closed his mind, concentrated on making his way back to Doc's place without tripping, only passing a few people who didn't pay him undue attention.

The company was still there and Jigger had got out of his bed and joined Septimus, the doctor and little Crip in the study. Crip was beginning to behave like one of the city fathers.

With Doc, Quest looked in on Buck, who lay very still, eyes closed in ashen face, breathing ragged.

Doc said he was worried about Buck, who should be in hospital, but of course Lobo Forks had no hospital. And maybe it would be too late to move the sick man now.

They went back to the study. 'You get your room fixed at Della's place?' Doc wanted to know.

'Hell, I forgot all about it,' Quest exclaimed. 'A feller turned up to visit Miss Polly.'

'Derry Saxe?'

'That's the one.'

'Can't see what Polly sees in that fancypants,' said Septimus, who had a humorous streak. That's the word, thought Quest, that's the right one to describe Derry. But was he more than that?

In a way, Crip answered the unspoken question. 'Friend o' big Cal's. Fancies himself as a *pistolero*. Haven't seen him in action though.'

Elias came in. He'd been to see his boys, as he called 'em, see they didn't get into trouble, fights they weren't paid for – to bed 'em down sort of – like an old aunt Septimus said.

There was a knock on the door. Doc asked Crip to go get it and, somewhat reluctantly, the little man did so. He was all smiles when he returned, however, for with him was Della, come to apologize for not showing Quest the room while he was at the shop.

'You shouldn't walk the streets this time of night,' Septimus told her with severity.

'It's only a hop, stride and jump.'

'I'll walk you back,' said Quest.

'Derry's gone,' she said. No more comment. A loyal person.

'It ain't late,' Elias said. 'You comin' back here, Obe?'

'Yes. In case Judge Cracker turns up.'

'I guess he won't be here till morning,' Septimus said.

The man and the girl were walking down the street when the thing happened.

Elias Slack had warned Quest. The elderly pugilist had said, 'You ain't marshal yet, so watch your back, bucko. Before an' after I mean, but mostly right now....'

'I ain't marshal,' Quest had said. 'You spoke up.'

'You will be, take my word for it. And there are plenty folks here who need a marshal about as much as they need a minie ball in the brain. Bucko, they don't want a marshal – and if they can get rid of a marshal before said gent actually becomes a marshal, if you see what I mean, they'll do just that. Less kick-back y' see – killing a lawman ain't exactly a rarity in these godless lands, I'll give you that, but when it happens it creates more stink than the death of a private citizen.'

'You talk too much,' Quest had told Slack.

But there you were...!

They came out of the darkness of an alley, the two of them, and there was nobody else around except the man they were after and the girl with him. And they both had guns and the one with the biggest gun – a sawn-off shot-gun no less – said, 'You make a peep or a quick move, pizen, an' the lady gets it in the belly.'

Della gave a little shocked sob, and the second

man said, 'Button it, lady. And you, Mr Tall, you
drop your hardware.'

Quest gave Della a would-be reassuring pat on
the arm and then he unbuckled his gunbelt and
let it fall.

'Come over here with me,' the man with the
shot-gun said.

His partner, who only had a big Colt, moved
aside to let the man and the girl get past him,
then he picked up the loaded gunbelt with his free
hand and slung it over his shoulder.

Then they were in the alley with the shot-gun
merchant, and the second man moved up behind
them as his pard said, 'Stick your hands in the
air.'

They did this; and the second man, with grunts
of triumph, relieved Quest of his Bulldog pistol
and even found the knife. They behaved like
professionals these two.

The man ran his hands over the girl, saying,
'You might have a little bitty knife or somep'n,
chiquita.' He looked like a Mexican at that, what
they'd seen of him.

The girl cursed him softly under her breath.
Quest's admiration for her grew: where'd she
learn such words?

Both the hold-up men laughed quietly, nastily.

'That's enough,' said the man with the shot-gun.
'Move, you two, side by side, quietly, not too fast.'

Perforce, they had to do as they were told. And
the two men picked their alley well. There didn't
seem to be anything each side of it but black, dark

walls. No light shone in from the street now. This
was a place used by cats and other animals: you
could smell 'em. There was grass; and the
footwear of the two people with their two captors
made little sound upon it.

They felt the breeze of the plains as they
reached the top of the alley and the man with the
shot-gun told them to turn left, which they did.
Then the man told them to stop and they were in
front of a closed door.

'Push it, *chiquita*,' said the sidekick with the
Colt.

Della reached out and pushed the door. It
wasn't fastened. It swung open. Beyond it was a
small wash of light which seemed to come from
another partially open door to which the two
captives were shepherded.

'Butt through,' said the man with the shot-gun.
A harsh voice, with a flavour of the Eastern
seaboard about it, Obadiah Quest thought.

Della was silent now, but she walked straight
through the second door with her head up as if she
were making an intended visit. Then they were in
a lighted room, coming to a halt, facing two more
men.

One in a chair with bandaged face and head was
the big feller called Cal. The other one, standing a
little to Cal's rear was the fancy younker called
Derry Saxe. It was his presence that brought a
gasp to Della's lips.

'You!' she cried.

Derry looked decidedly uncomfortable. He tried

to look tough also but didn't make a very good job of it.

Cal said, 'Why'd you bring the woman?'

The shot-gun man said, 'It was a chance too good to let by. Nobody about at all. You wanted 'im, you got 'im.' A jerk of the thumb in the direction of Quest.

'The woman's an extra,' said his dark-skinned partner. 'We won't charge for her, will we, *amigo*?'

'I guess not.'

The other man chuckled, not a nice sound though. 'I'll take care of little missy. She'll be my *chiquita*.'

'I didn't bargain for this,' said Derry Saxe in a strangled sort of voice.

'What are you doing here then, you snake?' snapped Della.

'She spits too,' said the dark man. 'I like that.'

'Shut your mouth, Chico,' said big Cal.

'Let her go,' said Quest. 'You want me. You've got me. Let her go.'

'Can't now, you must see that. Sorry.'

'Horse-shit!' It was a comparatively mild expletive: Quest had heard Della use worse.

'I ain't sort of conditioned now,' said Cal. 'And what's got to be done has got to be done mighty quick. That's somep'n else you must see.'

Quest was edging, playing for time. 'I don't see anything. Who the hell are you anyway? I ain't seen you here before. What are you doin', taking on this town?'

'Business, my man, purely business.'

Quest remembered that Elias Slack hadn't been able to remember Cal's surname, if he'd ever known it. He'd said he thought it was kind of foreign. Cal had an American Christian name, looked like a native American ... but, hell, the West was a melting pot for all kinds from all over....

'Who are you?' Quest asked again.

'My name is Beaucaire,' the big man said.

And now Quest knew. He'd heard that name before. And Elias said he'd heard that Cal had a rep down on the Pecos, that maybe the law wanted him down there.

'Cal Beaucaire of the Pecos,' Quest said.

A gunfighter almost as notorious as he was himself. Maybe even more so in other places. 'I didn't hear that Beaucaire made war on women.'

'A matter of expediency, my friend.'

Come to think of it, Cal didn't look like a gunfighter, didn't much talk like one either. Fancy! Judge Cracker would love him.... But would Judge Cracker ever hear anything from his old friend, Quest?

'I didn't figure on the woman,' said Derry Saxe weakly.

Cal didn't turn his head but looked straight at Chico and his shot-gun-toting friend and said, 'Take 'em out. Far out into the hills. Then do what you have to do, what you're being paid to do.'

'We allus do what we're paid to do,' said Shotgun.

Cal did turn his head then.

'You go with them.'

Derry said, 'I didn't aim....'

'I said you go with them! Do as you're told.'

The prisoners were shepherded out, the two gunnies behind them, Derry bringing up the rear.

They moved into the dark night and to where a small wagon with two horses were waiting behind a tall mound of rubbish which stank of many things. There was a buzz from the main street but they didn't see anybody.

Derry drove the horses. The other two, guns at ready, crouched in the back of the equipage with the prisoners. They took a trail out without passing through the town. There was a pale moon but the stars were mere pinpricks and there wasn't a lot of light.

12

Quest knew the hills. He had no doubt that Della knew them also. They were a long way away but could be reached while there was still night. Still, during the journey there might be a chance....

Derry was driving the horses as if devils were driving him: he was as fidgety as a fish on a slippery hook. And Cal, sitting back there in Lobo Forks like he owned the town, had Derry on some kind of a hook.

But Derry was a mighty uneasy feller and Della had added to this uneasiness by cussing him roundly at the beginning of the journey. She was quiet now, but maybe she was just getting her breath back.

The two horses were going like wildfire and the wagon rocked and swayed. The shot-gun man had already told Derry to be more careful, knowing that one of the prisoners would try for the gun if it was jerked from his grip. They were feisty ones, these two.

The man's pard Chico had his long-barrelled

Colt resting on his knee, pointing loosely at the prisoners who'd been made to sit closely together. But not too close. Even that might complicate things if one of them decided to behave recklessly.

The shot-gun man, whose name was Clem, didn't know the younker Derry very well, didn't want to know him much, was dubious about the way he was behaving. He'd heard the things that the yellow-haired girl had said to Derry. He was a friend of a friend of hers it seemed, and she figured he was acting traitor, had told him so in pungent and colourful terms.

It was a pity they had to put a pill to such a forthright filly, Clem thought. He knew Chico wanted a piece of her, and he had to admit now that he wouldn't mind some of that himself.

But Chico and he had a job to do and they always did the job they had to do all the way down the line, *completely*: they had a formidable rep for such doings. They planned to retire from the game when the trail got weary, and get themselves a ranch and a bunch of brainless cowhands to run it so they could spend their time in the sun on rocking chairs instead of on the back of a horse toting the armoury and doing the business.

He knew the notorious Obadiah Quest was watching him like a hungry hawk and not missing Chico either with those cold eyes. Clem had heard somewhere that Quest was reckoned to be the fastest gun alive and a merciless killer if it suited his book.

That'd suit his book all right now.

He wasn't saying anything though, wasn't nearly as gabby as the yellow-haired filly. She talked. He watched. And, somehow, they were both getting at Derry, who was using his whip on the horses as if he wanted to flay 'em alive.

'You'll wear them critturs out afore we get to them damn' hills,' Clem yelled.

Derry didn't seem to hear. Well, if he gets too awkward I'll shoot him as well as the other two, reflected Clem. Before them even. Or maybe it would have to be done anyway, shut that young jackass's mouth for good and round the job off neatly.

Shooting, that was the be-all and end-all of it, reflected Clem. Men like him lived by the gun, and there were many like him and his pard Chico, roaming the West, vying with each other to pick up the best jobs, using their gun-toting abilities. And was Obadiah Quest any better than he and Chico were? Hell, no, he was a paid killer too and one of the best. Maybe the best of all. But it didn't do to think about that now....

Clem was quick, and so was Chico. Clem didn't claim to be the fastest. Faster than Chico, or slower: he didn't know. He had heard of partners who were jealous of each other's abilities with shooters and it got so bad that finally they just had to find out who was best. Clem wondered if it would ever come to that between him and Chico.

Chico was as vicious as a half-skinned sidewinder but he loved living and booze and girls. Particularly girls. He was looking at that golden-haired filly as if he'd like to eat her.

Yeh, they were both good shots, he and Chico, Clem thought. And handy with knives, rope, adept with any kind of weapon you could mention, ordinary or otherwise.

Clem had seen Chico strangle a man with his own kerchief, his knees in the man's belly to keep him down while he choked to death. Clem himself had once pinned a fractious farmer – during a range war – to his own barn door with a pitchfork.

But fast? Hell, it wasn't the fastest who always got off the fatal shot to the other feller, not with the sort of big gun – Colt, Remington, Smith and Wesson, Adams, and other lesser-known hoglegs whether single or double-action, rimfire or whatever – freely available in the wide south-west.

Cal Beaucaire was fast. He was big and looked kind of clumsy and that fooled people. There were dead fools to prove it.

Back on the edge of the river plains of the Pecos a couple of years ago (and that was when he'd first met Cal) Clem had seen a bragging fool shot to rags by the big feller. The gunny had claimed to be the fastest ever; Cal had claimed plumb nothing: he'd shot the feller in several different parts of his anatomy before dispatching him with a bullet between the eyes.

Could Obadiah Quest be faster and more accurate than Cal Beaucaire...? But, hell, that question would never be answered now.

* * *

'I would've expected Obe to be back here by now,' said Elias Slack.

'He is kind of late,' said Doc Noah Keane, 'and we all ought to be in our beds.'

'Yeh, mebbe Obe's forgotten all about us an' gone to his bed,' said Elias. 'And when you consider that he went out of here with the lovely Della to her place....'

'There's no call for that,' snapped the plump medico.

'I didn't mean nothin' by it, Doc. Anyway, that other gal's there, ain't she, what's her name?'

'Polly.'

'Shall I go an' sort of make enquiries?' put in small Crip tentatively.

'I hope they haven't run into trouble,' said lawyer Septimus.

'Yeh,' said Elias and he didn't look humorous now, just anxious. 'I warned that tall man....'

'I don't mind going and looking,' said Crip with a show of bravado.

'All right,' said Elias. 'But watch yourself.'

'Don't I always?'

And that was a fact. Crip left the room. The others heard the outer door close behind him.

'I'm not tired,' said Septimus. 'I'll stay.'

'Me too,' said Elias.

'I live here,' said the doc sardonically. 'So it looks like we'll all stay. I'm not tired either. So I'll go look at my patient.' He quitted the room.

Buck Beckon was still out to the world. Doc thought his breathing might be a mite better. It didn't sound so loud in the stillness. Early days.... But would Buck survive the rest of the days?

Jigger was wideawake and sitting, gargoyle-like, upright in bed. 'Somep'n's going on. What's goin' on?' the young prizefighter demanded.

'We're just having a confab.'

'What about?'

'Nothing important. You go to sleep, my boy. If you want to mend quickly you need your rest.'

'I'm gonna get outa bed.'

'If you do I'll wash my hands of you.'

'Oh, all right,' said Jigger petulantly. He lowered himself in the bed and rolled over, showing Doc his back.

Keane returned to his other friends.

13

Main Street was empty, though Crip thought he saw figures in the distance. It was a dark night. There was still a sort of buzz in the atmosphere – that was the only way to describe it. The Dirty Ace would be near to closing, but the Golden Palace would still be going strong as gambling shifts came and went: many gamblers and dealers slept by day. The alley cribs would still be doing business also: their denizens were real night birds.

Crip passed nobody. He halted at the door of the millinery shop. He lifted the latch and pushed, wasn't surprised to discover that the door was locked. He rapped on it with his knuckles, trying to peer though the curtains covering the glass on the inside where there was a background glow.

He had to knock again before he heard the quick, soft footsteps. Then a voice he recognized called, 'Who's there?'

'It's me, Miss Polly. Crip. I'm looking for Mr Quest.'

The key was turned, the bolts drawn, the door opened. Plump, red-haired Polly wore a furry robe and moccasins.

She looked anxious as she said, 'You'd better come inside.'

He slipped through. She closed the door but didn't lock it, stood before it.

'I haven't seen Mr Quest since earlier tonight. And Della went out – I understood it was to see Mr Quest again. She hasn't come back. I haven't seen either of them.'

'They left the doc's place some time ago, we figured they'd come here.'

'They haven't.' Polly clasped her hands together.

'Have you any idea where they might be?'

'No, I thought you might....'

'No.' Crip hesitated. Then he said, 'I'll go look for them. I can't think....'

'Let me get some clothes on and then I'll come with you.'

'You shouldn't, Miss Polly.'

'If you don't wait for me I'll come after you.'

'Oh, all right.'

But she was leaving him. He stood by the door like a peddler with no place to go, and that was about the size of it, he thought.

When Polly returned quickly she had on a brown cloak and her abundant red hair was partially covered – in contrast to the drab voluminous garment – by a brightly, many-coloured Indian scarf.

She led the way out and locked the door behind her. Crip had been doing some quick thinking. He said, 'We'd better go back to the doc's place first to see if those two have turned up coming from another direction.'

'All right.'

As they turned in the direction they wanted, three men, obviously jettisoned from the saloon, ran into them.

'What you got there, Crip?' said one staggering big feller. He looked enormous to the little man as he stood in the boardwalk blocking their way, his friends posturing and chuckling in the background.

'It's a girl,' said one.

'I can see it's a girl,' said the other.

Crip didn't recognize any of the three of them. They were cowboys on their free time out on a toot, or drifters passing through town, picking up what they could on the way.

The last thought was a pretty sobering one. But it didn't sober the trio. They obviously had other things on their mind. The big one was the nearest and he reached for the girl.

He caught hold of the edge of her cloak and pulled her towards him, jerking her off-balance. She managed to swing at him with her fist but missed, and he yowled with laughter.

'Hey,' shouted Crip and started forward.

One of the other men hit him a hammer-like blow on the side of the head and he was propelled from the edge of the sidewalk. He hit the rutted earth hard and he blacked out.

The big man had the girl against the wall, had
her cloak open and was fumbling inside with his
big hands. She tried to knee him, managed to get
him, but only on the inside of his thigh, making
him hiss. But then he was laughing again.

She opened her mouth to scream but only
managed to make a small sound before one of his
hands clamped down over her mouth.

His two pards held the girl, one dragging at her
legs to bring her down. They weren't laughing
now; all three of them were panting like hungry
animals.

What they were about made them unaware of
the other three men who came up from behind,
closing in on them.

A smaller man, the furthest away from the girl,
was hit with a roundhouse blow that split his ear
apart and sent him to join Crip on the hard
ground as the latter, whimpering, began to come
around.

Another man was grabbed by the neck and
swung around and away from his big partner and
the struggling girl, was hit in the belly and, as he
doubled, was slammed full in the face. He hit a log
wall and slid down it to finish in a half-sitting,
half-reclining position with his head dripping
blood on to his shirt and his senses gone
completely.

The big feller turned away from the girl to face
Elias Stack, smaller, older, hunched but muscular
and fast and professional and loaded for bear.

Whether the big feller knew Slack from old was neither here nor there right then. The feller stood no chance anyway.

A right to one eye, a left to the mouth, a right to the belly and as the man bent, an uppercut to the descending underslug jaw. And Elias holding him with one hand so that he wouldn't buffet the distressed girl who was right behind him.

The big feller was tough, instinctively trying to cover himself. But it was a last dying stab at nothing. He was pulled away and slung into the street and he was still staggering as Elias went after him.

The other man who lay in the street was, as he rose, being attacked by Crip who'd turned into a wildcat, a flailing, spitting ball of fury. The drifter managed to elude the little man and took off down the street as if Satan himself was at his heels.

Crip sat in the middle of Main Street and gasped, and watched Elias work on the big feller as if he were a tree being felled. Elias, with cold fury, was meting out punishment that no man, taking it so terribly as this, would ever be able to forget.

But finally the thing was at an end and a bloody, senseless hulk lay still in the middle of the potholes and ruts on the hard ground.

Elias, misshapen, panting, arms hanging at his sides, was aware of Crip, said, 'It's a good job I figured I oughta come out too, and I picked up two of my boys on the way.'

The two boys were looking after the girl, but she

had a hold of herself now, said, 'I'll be all right.
That scum didn't hurt me much, didn't have time.
We have to find Della and Mr Quest.'

'It's a mystery,' mumbled Crip, rising to his feet.

'You all right, half-pint?' queried Elias.

The little man raised a bleeding face which
wasn't as pretty as it had been. 'I'll be fine,' he said.

'You go back into the shop and stay with Miss
Polly,' said Elias. 'We'll carry on from here after
we've put these two boys in the brig with the other
jasper, what's-'is-name…?'

'Randy Digo.'

'Yeh.'

Polly, completely on her feet now and standing
on the edge of the boardwalk, heard what was said
and had two cents' worth of her own to enter into
the conversation – bluntly. 'I'm coming with you.
Della's my best friend and now I'm mighty worried
about her. I just can't hang about and wait.'

'Me neither,' said Crip, who was full of surprises
lately. 'Della's my friend too, and so is Obe Quest.'

Elias eyed both of them in turn and they met his
gaze challengingly if, in the case of Crip, rather
lopsidedly. The old, humped, ex-prizefighter
shrugged, a strange movement, and said simply,
'All right.'

His two boys were hauling the two drifters up
as best they could. The third one was long gone.
They'd heard a galloping horse and figured that
that was the escaping boy, and they hadn't the
time to chase him so he was the lucky one.

Elias said, 'You boys do what you have to do and

then start looking. We'll start right away, Miss
Polly, Crip an' me. If you find anything ... well,
we'll have to have some meeting place I guess. Or
mebbe some kind of signal, huh?'

'I'll give out with the ol' coyote yip-yip,' said one
of the boys. 'You heard it, boss, ain't you, and it'll
sure echo round the town now, it bein' quiet here
now an' all?'

'It could wake some o' the town up,' said Elias.
'I've heard it all right. That time you got lost....'

The boy laughed. 'Fell over my own damn' feet
an' knocked my head an' wandered.'

'Well, all right, let's not waste any more time.
You give that signal if you have to an' the townies
will have to put up with it.' Elias turned to the
girl. 'You all right, Miss Polly?'

'I'm waiting,' said the redheaded girl sharply,
obviously almost distraught now with anxiety for
her friend, particularly after the horrendous
experience she herself had just suffered.

This came back to her: her voice changed as she
went on haltingly, 'If you hadn't turned up ... I do
purely thank you-all.'

'Weren't nothing, Miss Polly.'

'Naw.' The two boys were in unison.

The party broke up.

14

Were they at their destination now, and was this to be their rendezvous with death? They had stopped and Derry Saxe had got down from the seat of the wagon and Clem had said to the two captives, 'We'll light here, people.' And he appeared almost affable about it, as if this was a picnic they'd planned. A moonlight treat – though there wasn't much moonlight and surrounded by the hills as they now were, this was like the darkness of the grave.

Affable or not Clem still had his gun levelled, as did his partner Chico, whose white teeth shone as he grinned; and it was obvious that his eyes were fixed on Della, her every movement as, with Quest's help, she clambered down from the back of the wagon. And then Quest was in the way, and Chico didn't like that.

He hit Quest across the side of the head with the barrel of the gun and the tall man pitched sideways, away from the girl. It was a savage blow, bringing Quest to the ground, obviously half-stunned but still trying to rise as, with an inarticulate cry, Della ran to his aid, bent over him.

Chico grabbed hold of the girl and, as he did so, his gun was lax in his other hand.

Both Clem and Derry were starting forward, the latter with a sort of reluctance. They both had uplifted guns. But the explosion that awakened the echoes in the hills didn't come from either of those weapons.

Chico came backwards forcibly, his feet leaving the ground as he arched. His face was a white oval, but an incomplete one. The gun in Quest's hand, Chico's own gun, had blown part of Chico's head away. The bullet from the gun that, with a superhuman effort, Quest had snatched from the Mexican's hand as he grabbed the girl.

But now, even as Quest began to raise that gun again, Chico's pard Clem had his weapon levelled at the tall man whose reflexes had slowed as he fought his aching head. His first action in bringing about the lecherous Mexican's death had taken a lot out of him. Now Della and he looked death in the face.

'Goddam you,' said Clem from between clenched teeth. 'Now we're gonna bury you here. But first, tall man, I'm gonna shoot you to pieces, kill you slow.'

The echoes had died. But now they were reawakened. But the gun that spoke didn't speak from the fist of Clem. The report came from behind him, the bullet at close quarters driving

him forward to fall almost at the feet of his two
captives.

And Derry Saxe said, 'I wanted no part in this.'

'Drop the gun, *amigo*,' said Quest and the gun
in his own hand was levelled now and Della was
standing beside him and Derry was a clear target.

He dropped the gun. 'I saved you,' he said
weakly.

'What would you have done if things had gone
another way, though?' Quest said. A thin trickle of
blood ran down the side of his face, but he had a
hold of himself now.

'You're coming back with us,' he continued.
'You're driving the wagon back to town.'

'I'll do anything you say,' said Saxe. 'I'll tell you
anything you want to know.'

'You know a lot, huh?'

'I know enough.'

'First of all though, I have another job for you.'
Quest indicated the bodies. 'I want this carrion
covered up so that nothing can get at it, no sign
can be seen.'

Della sat on a rock, silent now, still. Quest had
Saxe's gun, held two guns now, kept them on the
young man collecting rocks, going about his grisly
task.

But eventually it was finished, and Saxe had
done a good job. He climbed on to the wagon seat
and Della and Quest got into the back.

The horses descended the winding slope
through the hills and were much more fidgety now
than when they'd climbed it earlier. Their ears

had been assailed by gunshots; they had smelled death. There had been dust and clatter, much activity. And the downward way was much more perilous.

The young driver was pushing them again even more than he'd done before. They smelled his uncertainty and his fear.

'We're gonna be dead, you an' me,' said Quest to the girl. 'Just like Cal Beaucaire wanted us to be. We're gonna be dead for a while.'

'But how...?'

'This boy's gonna be dead too – and the others have moved on.'

Half-turning his head, Saxe said shrilly, 'I promised...'

'Drive, boy!'

'You've got the money.'

'So? Have you got yours?'

'Not till I get back. Cal promised me.'

Saxe had stripped the bodies, buried the clothes separately. He had handed Quest back his weapons and the money he'd found in the clothing, quite a stash. But was that half the pay or all of it, pay in advance? Saxe didn't know. Quest had no means of telling.

Saxe was peeved that the two hired killers had had money up front and, so far, he'd had nothing. He sensed a double-cross that may have been planned for him by his own side. But corpses couldn't tell him whether this was likely or not.

Had Chico and Clem planned to finish Saxe too, with Quest and the girl? Had that been Cal

Beaucaire's plan also?

Had that rich stash been the two killers' pay in full and, a triple job done, had they been ready to ride off into the night laughing like loons who weren't planning to return to Lobo Forks nohow?

Was Derry Saxe ever about to see Lobo Forks again, or any other place for that matter?

What had Obadiah Quest meant...?

In the gloomy darkness of the night one of the horses suddenly balked at a queerly shaped clump of brush, for the strange light played strange tricks. The horse's hooves skittered and he banged into his mate and then they were both out of control, trying desperately to right themselves and snorting with terror.

In back of the wagon Della had the best perch, a benchlike appendage which allowed her to hold on to the side of the vehicle while it tossed on its rough passage.

Quest, however, wasn't so lucky. He squatted in the flat of the equipage and kept his gun handy in line with Derry Saxe's back.

Quest was thrown hard against the side of the wagon and the wood bent under the impact. The tall man was no lightweight. His weight carried him out of the wagon and he hit the ground hard. He felt his left arm go with a sickening snap and the pain was almost immediate, red hot, and shooting to his shoulder with an intensity that partially stunned him. It sickened him.

The gun he held had fallen inside the wagon. It was Saxe's gun. Quest's own gun had been returned to its holster. Instinctively he groped for it with his good right hand. The gun was still there, but he was in a strange position and waves of pain washed over him, buffeted him.

Derry Saxe had swung around and slipped into the flat of the wagon and Della and he were wrestling for the gun that Quest had dropped. The horses had come to a halt and, unhurt, stood trembling.

Saxe had grabbed for the gun but Della had managed to forestall him. She had the gun now and Saxe was trying to tear it from her.

His own gun out, Quest lurched to his feet, reaching the side of the wagon. 'Hold it,' he shouted thickly.

Derry Saxe was desperate now, mad. Suddenly he had the gun. He flung the girl away from him and she cannoned into Quest, knocking him from the edge of the wagon.

Man and girl rolled apart, Quest on his back, still holding his gun and fighting his way through waves of pain, raising the weapon. The shadowy, wavery figure of Saxe appeared leaning over the edge of the wagon, the gun glinting in his hand.

The gun blazed. The report was a deafening thing among the rocks. The bullet buzzed past Quest's ear, spanged against a rock and whined away in a ricochet. This was taken up by the boom of the weapon in Quest's hand.

The slug bored into Saxe's forehead and he was thrown backwards, disappearing in the bed of the wagon. He didn't rise again. Quest was professional enough to know that he'd got his man good. Della, shaken but unhurt, helped him to his feet. He leaned against the side of the wagon while, shuddering, she covered Saxe's body with an old tarp.

The horses were restive again. The wagon moved, almost throwing Della off her feet. She managed to reach the reins, grab them. The horses were reassured.

'You'll have to drive, honey,' said Quest. 'My left arm feels like it's busted.'

'Let me look at that first then, fix it as best I can.'

15

They had combed the town. Nobody had seen Obadiah Quest and the girl Della, either singly or together.

Della had been seen in the shop. Quest had been seen in the saloon, the gambling hall and in other places, as well as on the streets. But that had been some while ago and now most of the town slept, or tried to. The searchers weren't particularly quiet, and they wanted answers.

They gathered eventually on the edge of town. Elias Slack and his two boys, Della's friend Polly, little Crip. They had found nothing and no signal had been given, no coyote call to enliven them and quell their anxiety.

'Maybe they left town,' said Crip.

'Why would they do that without telling anybody?' said Elias.

'Yes, why?' asked Polly.

'No good quizzing me,' said Crip. 'How would I know?'

'Mebbe you know more than you think,' said Elias.

'Horse-shit,' said the little man, with none of his usual elegant if somewhat shifty manner.

He turned his head towards Polly. He had wiped his face and it wasn't so bloodied, but it looked lopsided in the night. 'Excuse my profane language, Miss Polly,' he said.

'I feel like cussing myself,' said the redheaded girl with her first sign of levity this night.

'We'll get horses and take a ride out,' said Elias. 'Me an' my two boys. Polly an' Crip, you stay here in case Della and Obe turn up.'

Somebody would have to do that of course. This time Polly and Crip didn't argue about it. Crip said he had a splitting headache. Polly said she'd get him something for it.

Elias and his two boys, horsed at last, weren't sure which direction to take, didn't know whether the journey would be of any use after all.

They went towards the hills hidden by the night. Although Elias didn't say so to his companions he was beginning to fear that some foul play might have taken place. Quest was a target. But the girl ... what about the girl?

They were way out on the plains and hadn't seen any moving thing and the sky was lightening when one of the boys said he thought he heard hoofbeats.

'Mebbe Polly an' Crip changed their minds,' said Elias caustically. 'Wimmen are allus changing their minds. I ain't no great admirer of that little cuss Crip but I guess he wouldn't let the girl come on her own.'

'No,' said the boy, who was a fighter rather than a rider and was feeling some discomfort. 'The sound was in front not behind.'

They reined in their horses and they all listened.

They all heard it then. The sound of hooves – and maybe the rumble of a wagon's wheels.

'Who could that be so early in the mornin'?' said Elias.

Approaching dawn was pinkening the sky. The three horsemen couldn't see the hills yet but they could see more in front of the rolling plains and they saw the equipage, the horses. And they drew their guns, a concerted reflex action after an anxious night.

They waited.

The sharp-eyed boy lowered his gun. 'It's them,' he said.

Elias craned his head forward, said 'Godamighty, so it is.'

All three of them sheathed their guns. They kneed their horses forward to meet the wagon with the two horses, the two people seated side by side on the seat.

Conversation was garbled at first. Quest had his arm in a sling, cloth torn from the bottom of Della's petticoat.

Question and answer. Finally their story mainly told.

'The arm ain't as bad as I thought it might be,' said Quest.

'How's it feel then?'

'Like a nagging tooth. An' I can stand that.'

'This beats all,' said Elias. 'We've had trouble in town too.'

And that was the other story.

Della was relieved to hear that her friend Polly was unharmed, and even that little Crip had only received small injuries to his handsome boy's face, nothing serious.

They were turned about. 'We've got to get you to the doc, Obe,' said Elias.

'We're dead, Della and me,' said Quest. 'For the time being that is. Till Judge Cracker turns up an' swears me in as marshal. It's a pity it's daylight now. We don't want to get spotted.'

'If you both get in the back of the wagon we'll cover you,' Elias said. 'Derry Saxe ain't gonna mind.'

The macabre joke fell flat. 'Oh, God, Mr Slack,' said Della. 'I think Polly's going to mind – but I don't know how much.'

'Was she very taken with him?' Elias asked.

'They were friends. He visited the shop a lot. But I don't know how much she was taken, as you put it.'

'His death will be put under wraps for a bit,' said Quest. 'Give you time to break it to her gently. You can trust her, can't you?'

'Of course.'

'Let's do what Elias suggested then.'

'All right,' said Della, if somewhat reluctantly it seemed, which was hardly surprising. The wagon flat wasn't very big and having to share it with a corpse was no pleasant prospect, though she'd have a live man to keep her company also.

A couple of saddle blankets were produced. Elias's two boys unceremoniously shifted Saxe's body as far over to the edge of the wagon as possible and Della and Quest took the other side, close together, a blanket apiece.

Before the two had their heads covered Elias said, 'Mebbe we ought to bury young Derry out here anyway. Whadyuh say, Obe? Me an the boys 'ull do it.'

'No. I want him for evidence.'

'I hope he'll keep a while then,' said Elias before whipping up the blanket over his old sparring partner's head.

Della had already covered herself completely. Things – and the conversation – were getting a mite too gruesome for her taste.

The wagon rolled on with its escort.

The morning was balmy now. The sun not too hot, there was a gentle breeze.

The buildings of Lobo Forks came into sight, looking as still and peaceful as a cluster of churches. Nothing moved.

'We'll go round the back,' said Elias, directing the younker in the seat beside him.

They pulled up finally behind the doc's place, not having seen a soul. The smoke of breakfast was issuing from some chimneys but nobody yet seemed to be using the rows of privies. An early-prowling cat eyed the wagon and horses curiously from a rubbish dump.

They had to get Doc Noah Keane up. He was alone except for Buck Beckon and Jigger and they were both sleeping. Quest's query about his cousin was met with the little rotund man's usual laconicism. Doc was an optimist, but he wasn't a liar.

He had heard part of the story from Crip who'd paid him another quick visit last night. He was now told the rest. He said Septimus Lagg had gotten very tired and he (Keane) in his capacity of a medico had told his old friend to get home and to bed.

'He'll be back.'

'The less folks know about us being back the better it'll be,' Quest said.

Della said, 'I'd like to stop and get breakfast for you folks but I must go see Polly first.'

'Crip's with her, watching over her,' Doc said.

'I don't know about that little feller,' said Elias Slack dubiously.

'I'll come with you, Della,' said Quest. 'I can handle Crip.'

'I ain't only a sawbones,' said the doctor. 'I can cook too, and I always make my own breakfast.'

'Of course you do,' said Elias. 'But I'll help you this morning as there's so many of us. I can fight, but I can cook as well. Only thing I'm worried about is Della and Obe getting to the shop without being spotted now the town is waking.'

'Disguise,' said one of the young pugilists brightly.

Doc had an Indian woman who came and 'did'

for him, though spasmodically. She also took advantage of the surgery's washing facility. Doc had had a big fire-boiler installed. Absentmindedly, the woman had left some voluminous Indian blankets behind.

Doc had a suggestion which caused merriment. But grimmer things were yet to be discussed and Elias brought these up; Elias and his black sardonic humour.

'Derry Saxe'll have to be toted to the undertakers if we want to keep him only halfway fresh. The feller's got a big ice place.'

'We'll take the wagon,' said Quest. 'I'll tote the body to the morgue after I've dropped Della off. Petey is an old friend of mine.'

Petey Jakeson was the local undertaker, a man who shared Elias's sardonic sense of humour.

'Fine peggin',' said Elias. 'Where are those damn' blankets, Doc?'

'Oh, great Jehosophat,' said Obadiah Quest.

16

Two Indian ladies in voluminous blankets which covered them from head to toe drove a wagon and two horses along the 'backs' of Lobo Forks. A couple of folks saw them. A man came out of the privy and wanted no truck with Injuns, either male or female. And a fat housewife throwing swill over her littered apology for a house-yard, said, 'Good morning' and received twin grunts in return.

Quest dropped Della at the back door of the millinery shop and didn't drive on until a delighted Polly appeared. He'd already told Della 'Tell Crip to stay put till I see him.'

Petey, the undertaker, had just got up and offered his old friend Obe a cup of coffee. Petey made the best coffee in town, thick enough to revive the dead, some folks said, though it never had.

Having never seen Obe in an Indian blanket before Petey was beside himself with merriment. He almost dropped the corpse – his end anyway –

as he helped his big filly Injun friend to carry it
into the undertaking parlour and through that to
the big leanto where the ice-place stood.

Petey was somewhat of an engineer and had
had a spell on the new railroads, but he was better
at what he did now he said. He was a
perfectionist. He could make a corpse look like it
was ready to sit up and kiss folks.

'That was mighty fine coffee, old friend,' said
Quest as he left. 'I'll see you soon.'

'You'd better, bucko, I ain't no magician.'

Quest, wrapped in his blanket once more and
shuffling like a squaw, climbed into his wagon.
Petey was watching him from the kitchen window
and grinning like a maniac cat.

Quest drove the wagon to the back of the
millinery shop where Polly had left the door
unlocked and he slipped inside. He shut the door
and flung his voluminous garment away from
him.

The last thing he wanted was little Crip falling
about and laughing like a loon.

But Crip, greeting him, was as sober as a
hanging judge and full of arrogance at having
protected 'Miss Polly' from whatever other harm
might be awaiting her in this wild town.

Polly was sober too. Evidently Della had told
her of the fate of Derry Saxe. But neither girl
mentioned the fact to the new arrival. They were
making breakfast. Quest was persuaded to stay.

That young hellion Saxe had lived a sort of
double life, Quest reflected, and he wondered

again about the relationship between the young feller and redheaded, homely-featured Polly. Maybe Saxe's feelings for that girl had been as genuine as Quest's were for Polly's friend Della (there was a thought!) and you had to give him sad and belated credit for that.

They had finished breakfast and Quest and Crip were smoking a cheroot apiece, sitting across from each other at the kitchen table like bosom friends. The girls were doing chores. The back door was rapped. Polly opened it, turned her sad face away from the door and said, 'It's somebody for you, Mr Quest.'

It was one of Elias's boys, who said, 'An old feller called Judge Cracker has arrived at the doc's place and is asking for you, Mr Quest.'

'He's earlier than I thought he'd be,' said the tall, flame-haired man, rising.

But the news was welcome nonetheless.

'Don't forget your blanket,' said the boy with a small smile.

'Can I come with you?' asked Crip, but glancing at Miss Polly.

'We'll be all right,' she said.

With the men out of the way she'll be able to work off her feelings as women can, Quest reflected. The three men left.

It was good to see old walrus-moustached Cracker. By this time the others had put him in the picture pretty well and he knew what was expected of him, was more than willing to go along with it.

The battered Jigger had at last been allowed to get up. He sat in the old, rickety but most comfortable armchair in the study where the company was now gathered. Jigger had said he wasn't going to follow the pugilistic career any more. Doc Keane had already advised him against it. He had some *dinero* saved and was going to get himself a little spread. Maybe he'd find a nice girl too, get married.

His old friend and mentor, humpbacked Elias told him that if he needed any more capital he knew where to come. The company wasn't too surprised to learn from Jigger then that storekeeper and part-time prizefighter Pecos George had earlier made the same offer to the young man. After all it had been George who, if only indirectly, had put an end to Jigger's life with the maulies.

'He also offered me work in his store if I wanted,' said Jigger.

'You could take that for the time being,' said Elias.

'I might do just that.'

Judge Cracker had looked in on Buck Beckon, who was still dead to the world. Quest knew that the old man, who had tried to dissuade him from coming after Buck in the first place, would be wondering what would happen between Obe and Buck if the latter survived. But it wasn't a question Cracker would ask his young and valued friend Obe while among the present company, or any other company at all for that matter.

The swearing-in procedure was dead simple, and there were plenty of witnesses. Judge Cracker had even brought a badge with him which, although no example of the badge maker's best art, was pretty adequate. A silver shield with the word 'marshal' very plainly displayed under what appeared to be the small scratched illustration of a buffalo's head – or an ugly steer maybe, as Elias said after donning steel-rimmed spectacles and peering closely at it.

But Cracker added a sober note to the proceedings when he said, 'I hope there won't be any unnecessary killings.'

'Everything will be done proper an' legal, old friend,' said Quest. 'If with some trickery to even the odds.'

Cracker still looked a mite dubious but had no further comment to make.

Quest went on, 'Pity that young jasper, Derry Saxe got himself shot. It was 'im or me, as the skunk said to the wildcat. But if Derry had lived I figured he'd talk his head off an' tell us a thing or two.'

'I can tell you things, Obe,' said small Crip suddenly.

'I thought maybe you could, *amigo*,' said the new marshal, leaning forward in his chair.

Judge Cracker had got his sense of humour back. 'You're supposed to be dead, Obe,' he said. 'I haven't ever sworn in a dead man before.'

'He's a healthy boy,' said Doc Keane. 'But right now, new shiny badge or no new shiny badge, he ain't as fit as he should be.'

'I feel fine,' Doc.'

'Horse-feathers! You need rest. You need sleep. You're gonna go to bed. And I want you to rest that arm, give it time to heal properly. I want it to get back straight not crooked.'

'I've got a good right arm.' Quest knew he was goading the irascible little medico, but somehow he couldn't resist it.

'I know about you and your good right arm and what you can do with it, what you aim to do with it. But you'll do as I say first, that's if you want to operate properly. Or maybe you'd rather finish up dead, badge and all, the way the judge thought you might....'

Cracker began, 'I didn't exactly...'

But Doc was in full spate, and he hadn't finished yet. 'I've got another spare cot here and you'll take it.'

Elias interrupted now with his few cents' worth. 'My boys will keep an eye on the millinery shop and, if Della stays outa sight like you planned....'

'She will.'

'Of course. Then you do as the doc says now.'

'Now you're ganging up on me. All right, I'll go.'

'I'll show you,' said Doc Keane, mollified. His rotund form skipped in front of the tall man.

Quest looked in on Buck, Doc rising on his tiptoes to see past.

The patient was still sleeping. 'Give it time.' It was a whisper. *'Give it time.'*

Time, thought Quest. *But not too much time.*

He got into the comfortable cot. Yes, they all needed sleep, and he no less than the others. Doc was a wise old bird.

Because of his damaged arm the tall man had to lie in an awkward position. Also the cot wasn't quite long enough for him.

Despite his weariness he couldn't slumber immediately. He lay thinking of what had to be done next.

Not too much time!

He still had to listen to what Crip had to tell him.

He must have been still cogitating on this when sleep hit him like a hammer.

When he awoke the sun was streaming in through the window, bathing him in light and heat. He swung his feet out of bed. Although he didn't remember having done so he had divested himself of his boots, his leather vest and kerchief. His gun rig was on the chair beside the cot.

Groggily, he got himself shipshape again, using one hand most of the time. Doc had strapped his arm up. It ached with nagging spite. He tried to take Doc's advice and not move it much and only in an experimental way

He felt sharper. The house was quiet. He left the room. The quietness of the dead, he thought. A sobering thought.

He opened the neighbouring door. His cousin Buck Beckon had his eyes open, had even been able to prop himself up a little.

'Mornin', Obe,' he said.

17

Crip was still in the study curled up in an armchair. He awakened, rubbing his eyes like a petulant child, greeting Quest grumpily.

'Where's Doc?'

'He's downstairs.' Crip brightened. 'Early patient. Feller fell out of a bedroom window.'

'Was it his own bedroom window, that's the point?'

'Dunno ... Elias sloped off with his boys, said he'd soon be back. He's gathering them together I guess, but I reckon they're still staying in town.'

'I reckon,' said Quest.

'Did I hear you talkin' to Buck?'

'You did.'

'That's fine, mighty fine.'

'Yeh.'

Quest, as noncommittal as ever. Crip rising, stretching his small neat body. The bruises on his face were fading and he looked bright-eyed and mischievous again.

'There's just the two of us here now,' said the

other man. 'And you promised to tell me all you know about things that are going on in town, why Beaucaire wanted me so soon dead, and was willing to have the girl killed too. Things ain't right in this town, are they?'

'They never have been what you call right,' said Crip. 'You know that, don't you?'

'I guess.'

'It's always been an outlaw town with no real law, except that from time to time folks made their own. All kinds of folks came through here or stayed a while and moved on, sometimes law from outside on their tails. But in the main very few folks interfered with the regular townies like me and you, when you decided to stay awhile. Folks on the run never like to draw too much attention to themselves, do they? They want to hide, rest up, get help if they need it....'

Crip was in full flow, becoming breathless though. He paused. He looked at Quest with earnest blue eyes as he went on, 'There were always people to help 'em hide, succour them, feed them – at a price of course. But none of this was ever what you might call organized. Not till Cal Beaucaire turned up....'

Crip paused again, but this time it was obviously for dramatic effect.

But Quest looked totally unsurprised, said, 'Go on.'

'Beaucaire is into everything. And he's been getting gunnies in from elsewhere to help him. That feller Jeff that Buck killed was one of

Beaucaire's boys.'

'That figures.'

'Beaucaire and his boys, they *infiltrate*, that's what you'd call it, isn't it?'

'I guess.'

Quest suddenly wondered where Judge Cracker was: he must ask Crip. But Crip was going on again and Quest listened.

'Beaucaire and his boys have got themselves concessions at the Dirty Ace and at the Golden Palace and at other places. They're running the whores. They're running the hidey-holes and outlaws are coming in more than ever lately and using the places, and paying big for the privilege, and Beaucaire is taking the cream off the top of everything. He's taking, Obe, taking all the time. He's taking by intimidation, by fear. And folks who get in his way are disappearing. Just as you were supposed to disappear. And Miss Della too, because she happened to be in the way. Hell, a marshal in this town is the last thing Beaucaire and his sort wants.'

'I know.'

'So you've got something up your sleeve now, huh?'

'Sort of.' But Quest didn't tell the little man what and, knowing Obe of old, Crip didn't ask.

There were footsteps. The door opened and Judge Cracker entered.

He'd been staying with his old friend Septimus Lagg in that worthy lawyer's place just down the street. Septimus was better than he'd been yesterday when, as Cracker had been told, Sep had been kind of sick. But he'd be around soon.

'You haven't got your badge on.'

Quest put it on.

'How's the arm?'

'Mending.'

The judge was doubtless wondering just what Quest aimed to do next, and when. But he didn't ask either: he knew Obe even better than Crip did.

They sat and smoked and Doc Keane came in.

'How was the patient?' Crip asked.

Doc chuckled. 'Jack Tyker....'

'I know him.'

'He's been having a thing with Ike Bernet's missus while Ike's been out on the ranches breaking horses. I guess the whole town knew about it before Ike did.'

'I've known for weeks,' put in Crip.

'You would! Well, Ike came home unexpected. I might as well tell you all about it, the whole town'll know before the end of the day I'll wager. Jack hightailed it out of the bedroom window, busted his collar bone. He ought to rest up but he won't. Whether he'll try and leave town I don't know but, whether or not, if I know Ike Bernet, Ike's going to be after him.'

'Looks like you might need that badge sooner than you expected,' said Judge Cracker.

He and Quest exchanged glances and the latter said, 'Could be.'

'Let me look at that arm,' said Doc Keane.

'I know Ike Bernet,' said Quest. 'He ain't the sort to start shootin' up the town because he thinks folks ain't been straight with him. But he'll have to go after Jack Tyker I guess. Any man would.'

Cal Beaucaire was sitting at a table in a corner of the Dirty Ace Saloon. He was alone. He could see into Main Street from a window at his side but was pretty well hidden unless he craned himself forward.

He saw one of his boys cross the street, heard him clatter on to the sagging boardwalk.

The batwings swung open and the man came in, looking about him. Widening his eyes in the gloom after the brilliant sunshine outside. Beaucaire disdained to make a signal. But the man spotted him and came over, plopped down on the other chair at the small round table. He was out of breath.

'What the hell's the matter with you?' Beaucaire demanded.

The man fought for breath and won, said, 'I just saw Obe Quest. Wearing a badge an' all.'

'Bullshit!'

'Honest, Cal. Along the backs. I thought he went in through Ike Bernet's back door.'

Beaucaire laughed out loud. 'Another of Miz Bernet's fancy men, that's what you saw.'

'It was Quest I tell you.'

'Quest's dead an' buried. And there ain't any marshal in Lobo Forks.'

'I swear. I saw…'

'Mebbe it was Quest's ghost you saw. You been on the sauce early, Nat?'

'I ain't had a drop yet, Cal. An' I didn't have much last night either. I bin havin' trouble with my gut – somep'n I ate I guess.'

'That's it. An' it's gone to your damned head an' you're gettin' hallucinations or somep'n.'

'It was Quest I tell you.'

'Was there anybody else about?'

'Er – I – I don't think so…. But it was Quest. He'd got a sort of sling on his one arm. But it was Quest all right. I know. Nobody walks quite like him. Like a goddam cat.'

Beaucaire looked at him, looked at him very hard, not speaking now.

A bad arm! That had given him pause for thought. Derry Saxe hadn't yet returned from the hills. But, knowing the murderous nature of the two hired killers, Clem and Chico, Beaucaire hadn't worried overmuch about young Derry's non-appearance. Maybe that was for the best anyway.

But had the job been bungled somehow?

It didn't seem likely. Clem and Chico had a rep for reliability.

But Quest had a rep too. A cunning, fast, clever killer! *Back*?

But where was the girl?

'I want you to go the the millinery shop, Nat, Della an' Polly's place.'

The other man's eyes started in astonishment.

'Buy some pins or somep'n,' said Beaucaire. 'I want to know if Della's there.'

'But...'

'Do as I say. But be discreet.'

He watched Nat go, hoped the idiot wouldn't make a mess of what, to his boss, seemed a simple task. Sitting thinking. Hell, it didn't make sense....

But, with a curly wolf like Quest....

Beaucaire rose. But he didn't want to show himself outside yet. He sat down again.

He was relieved when two more of his boys came in. He didn't think he had ever been so pleased to see those two. Partners. Brighter than Nat.

'I want you to go an' watch Ike Bernet's place. One at front, one at back.'

'Ike's out lookin' for Jack Tyker,' said one of the boys. 'Did you hear?'

'I heard.'

The two boys left and Beaucaire was alone with his thoughts again. The new law of Lobo Forks had already got itself a tough, improvised hoosegow and three men were in there, one of them being a Beaucaire ally, crazy Randy Digo.

Beaucaire knew that the other two men in the blockhouse were drifters who had attacked milliner Polly and had been captured by Elias Slack and his boys.

Beaucaire didn't need drifters like that, and he sure as hell didn't need that humpbacked, prizefighting troublemaker Elias: that one's present sojourn in Lobo Forks was an added complication to say the least.

Nat came in, crossed to the table, said, 'Ain't nobody in the milliners' shop 'cept Polly herself. But she seems kinda fidgety.'

'She would be, wouldn't she, if her partner's missing?'

But was she: was Polly's partner Della still missing? Nat was an idiot, face like a sleepy heifer, mouth opening again and more words coming out.

'I saw Beal an' Coolie.'

'They're watching Ike Bernet's place.'

'I heard about Bernet, an' Miz Bernet, and Jack Tyker.'

Nat began to chuckle. Beaucaire cut him off. 'You join 'em. Join Beal an' Coolie.'

'Why? I thought...'

'Never try and think, Nat. Do as you're told.'

'You're the boss, Cal.' Nat turned away. The batwings swung behind him.

I should've told him to round up all the boys, thought Beaucaire. He sat.

No good going off half-cocked though. He'd wait for developments. Such as they may be. He poured himself another drink.

He didn't know that other boys were being rounded up – at the behest of Elias Slack.

18

All Quest found at the house was a weeping woman who had locked herself in a room upstairs and wouldn't come out until she heard who the caller was. He had heard her caterwauling from way down in the kitchen, having come in through the back door which had been left partially open.

Folks had left that abode in a hurry, one from the door, one from the upstairs window. Pity Ike Bernet hadn't caught up with Jack Tyker at Doc's place where he might've been reasoned with or something.

Now Ike was on Jack's tail and might kill Jack if he caught up with him. At the least Jack might finish up with something a damsight worse than a busted collar bone. Quest thought he knew how Ike felt. But law was law, and he (Quest) was the law now and he was stuck with it, had made his oath, was committed to upholding the law and enforcing it.

Already the comely woman's manner was changing at the sight of the tall man with the

wealth of red-gold hair and the steady blue eyes.
Still her indiscretion had been a setback to the
marshal's original purpose, a nuisance. He told
her to get back upstairs and lock herself in again
and not come out till he, or somebody else
speaking for him, called her again.

'I'm scared, Marshal. But if you stay with me....'

'Can't, ma'am. Duty calls....' He broke off too.

She pouted. She was a mighty fine pouter, he
had to give her that. But she turned away. He
listened to her climbing the stairs. Too damn'
slow. But finally the bedroom door closed behind
her and he heard her turn the key in the lock.

A locked bedroom door, a door with a lock on it
upstairs in a western house, that wasn't usual.
But maybe from time to time Ike had had to lock
her in himself.

Maybe this wasn't the first time that filly had
had herself a time with another man. Maybe Ike
would cool off and let the new Lobo Forks' law get
on with its more important business.

He made for the back door which he'd closed
behind him. But then instinctively he paused and
glanced through the window beside the door. A
man was out back watching the place. A hardcase
Quest had seen before, probably a Beaucaire man.

Quest backed away, turned, went through to
the front of the house.

Another hardcase was watching the front, was
being more discreet than his pard out back, was
trying to hide behind an unhorsed wagon, leaning
against it nonchalantly and smoking.

But he was suddenly accosted by a third man and there was some jawing and gesticulating before the newcomer stayed put and they both tried to hide themselves, not too successfully.

There were not many folks on the street right now, as far as Quest could see. But, suddenly again, two more men appeared and Quest recognized two of Elias Slacks' young pugilists.

That Elias! He didn't miss a trick. Quest hadn't wanted too many folks involved in his law business – not unless they were duly sworn-in deputies (and that would take time) – but he was glad of this intervention now. And intervention it certainly was. The fighting boys were looking at the other two like they'd welcome any interest – and the others returned those looks shiftily, uncertainly.

Quest went back to the kitchen, the window. The third man was still on his lonesome.

Quest went through the door.

The man had been half-hiding behind a leaning privy, maybe because he didn't want to be spotted smoking on the job, his awareness in temporary abeyance. The sudden appearance of Marshal Quest took him by surprise. He dropped his smoking cigarette from his right and hooked that hand for his gun-butt.

Quest's draw was smooth and easy. 'Hold it, friend,' he said. 'Or I'll blow your head off.'

The man froze in a grotesque parody of suspended action.

'Now reach over with your left hand and take out that shooter using two fingers only.'

The man did as he was told.

Awkward. But he made it. His gun hit the ground with a soft thud.

'Come over here.'

An obedient dog. 'Open that door an' go on through.'

Shuffle-shuffle. 'Lie down on your belly.'

Tricks. But nothing untoward. Nice doggy tricks.

Quest found towels, trussed the obedient dog. Like a turkey now; gagged too.

Quest was grinning. He should've slugged that feller, bust his head, left him lying. But he was law now, a marshal again and, by his lights, was playing it by the book. He climbed the stairs, knocked on the bedroom door. Already, hearing his footsteps, the woman was turning the key, getting ready to welcome him, all set probably.

'No need to open the door, ma'am,' he called. 'I just came up to tell you there's a man in your kitchen but he's quite harmless, trussed, can't even move.'

He went back down the stairs and she was calling after him. He didn't know whether she'd opened the door; he didn't catch the words.

He had a thought. Maybe she'd come down and let that feller go. Silly man-mad bitch. He decided to let it go at that, went through to the front of the house again, the front window.

The four men were all by the unhorsed wagon now. Quest went through the door, crossed the street. The two pugilist boys had their guns out, had the other two's gunbelts and armoury at their feet.

'They spoke out of turn, Marshal,' said one grinning boy.

'Congratulations an' thanks,' said Quest. 'You know where to put 'em, huh?'

'We do.'

Well, this was better, this happening. 'Take 'em round the back o' the house. There's another customer in the kitchen. I tied him up. Untie him an' take 'im with you. If that loco woman's downstairs, take her upstairs an' lock her up.'

'Right, Marshal.'

'On second thoughts, I'll come with you, don't want to show myself out front here yet.'

The woman was still upstairs, sulking no doubt. So things were uncomplicated. While the two boys marched their three prisoners to the blockhouse Quest continued on to look for Ike and Jack, hoping they wouldn't stage a fight in the middle of Main Street for all to see, that would blow the new marshal's cover all to hell, him having to take a hand and all!

He heard shooting from the opposite direction to the one the boys (his voluntary deputies) had taken their prisoners. He began to run. Awkward on his high-heeled riding boots over the lumpy and littered earth of the backs of town, his wounded arm jarring, pain stabbing; cursing between his teeth.

Ike had Jack cornered in an alley near the local whorehouse which was kind of appropriate, Quest thought. If Jack had gone there in the first place instead of poaching in somebody else's patch the local law wouldn't be having all this unnecessary trouble now.

Ike was crouching behind a barrel at the top of the alley. Jack was at the other end, peeping around a corner. He was all through running it seemed, busted collarbone and all. Quest, a punished man himself, thought he knew how Jack felt, even began to have a sneaking sympathy for Jack. He himself had never had to jump from no upstairs window – but he'd come pretty close to it a time or three.

He kept his hands away from his gun and he pointed a finger at the crouching Ike and snarled, 'Put it away for Chrissakes. Whadya think you're doing?'

Ike did as he was told, purely a reflex action, watched bemusedly as the new marshal marched down the middle of the alley, yelling, 'Hold your fire, you jackass.'

Jack came slowly around the corner, his gun dangling in his free hand. His other arm was in a sling very like the sling that Quest toted, having been fixed by the same person. But Quest, though he didn't seem aware of it now, had pulled his arm free from his sling and held it bent, if rather awkwardly.

Truth was, he was right now so boiling mad that he wasn't feeling any pain.

'Come together, you two,' he said, turning and beckoning to Ike.

Ike shambled forward, his hands free. Quest glared at Jack and Jack holstered his gun, pointed a finger at Ike.

'He's drunk as usual.'

'I ain't drunk,' retorted Ike. He badly needed a shave, and his eyes were bloodshot.

'He doesn't look after his woman. He's drinkin' all the time. He's turning into the town drunk.'

'You'll look after my woman for me, won't you, you son-of-a-bitch?' Ike started forward, his fists clenched.

Quest stepped in the way. He jabbed a finger at his chest, at his badge. 'Y'see this? I guess mebbe it's only tin. But it means somep'n. And while I'm wearing it you take notice of it, y'understand?'

'Sure, Obe, but....' This was Ike. He sounded almost tearful. Was he turning into a maudlin drunk?

'Hell, I thought you two were friends.'

'We used to be,' said Jack.

'He thinks he can...'

'He's drinking all the time, that's why his woman messes with other men. Besides, she ain't no...'

'Don't you go slanging....'

Ike didn't finish his sentence, moved again, staggered a little. Quest held him, said, 'That's right, Jack. Don't hide behind a woman, specially as she ain't your own.'

'Hell's bells. I ain't. Me an' Ike been pards since we wuz tads. We shouldn't fall out over some frail. Shootin'. Hell, I could allus shoot better'n Ike, and he ain't in any fit state now to...'

'Don't you go callin' my woman names.'

'I was just…'

'Keep away from her.'

'All right.'

But both of them, glowering, were now trying to get past Quest. His bad arm was getting punished by their jostling. He used his good right arm and pushed them apart furiously. 'That's enough! I've had enough, y'understand? If you want to fight, you can fight, but you don't use guns or any weapons. As soon as you're fit, Jack, I'll fix a bout with Elias Slack. A straight-up one. And you keep sober, Ike, I want no advantage on either side. That's my verdict, the law's verdict. It's either that or the hoosegow for both o' you.'

'I'll fight 'im any time he's ready,' said Ike.

'I'll be ready.'

But Ike was turning away, walking back down the alley, keeping his unsteady dignity, almost bumping into Elias Slack as Slack came round the corner.

'What was that, what was all the shooting?'

'I'll tell you about it,' said Marshal Quest.

19

Later, Elias said, 'Do you know what Ike's missus was afore he had her?'

'Nope.'

'He met her in a whorehouse down on the border. She was the only Anglo frail there, was supposed to be the *duenna* or somep'n for the rest of the girls, though she was no older herself than most of 'em.'

'I see what you mean,' said Quest. 'Hardly seems likely, huh? *Duennas* are usually ladies goin' on in years. Old maiden aunts an' that sort of thing.'

'So she was mebbe a workin' *duenna*,' said the humpbacked ex-prizefighter mischievously. 'It's likely I guess. That was the consensus around these parts, particularly with folks who already knew that hellhole of a border town – its name escapes me. But Ike brought her home an' married her.'

'An attractive lady.'

'Yeh. No wonder the boys gather round her like

she was honey in her jar with the top off. Jack
Tyker wasn't the first, not by a long shot. And you
know what I think, Obe?'

'Not rightly.'

'I think Ike's known all along. That's why he's
been drinkin' so much. But Jack was his friend,
mebbe his best friend, an' that was the unkindest
cut of all.'

'I get you.'

'Still and all, mebbe in the end they'll call off
that fight. Would you let 'em do that, Obe?'

'I guess so, if they want to go on that way, an'
Jack keeps away from the woman.'

'I think he will.'

'I ain't no arbitrator over domestic doings. I've
got more important things to think on.'

'You surely have, *amigo*. I don't think Cal
Beaucaire will stay fooled. Mebbe, with boozy Ike,
it'll soon be all around town that you're back an'
far from dead.'

'I reckon.'

'So you've got to move faster than you planned.
An' me an' the boys are right behind you, if you
want us.'

'I'll let know, *amigo*. You certainly got my bacon
saved at Della an' Polly's place.'

'No matter. And I'll tell you somep'n else.'

'What's that?'

'I told Buck that you were having a rethink
about the other thing. What do you say about
that, bucko?' Now Elias wore his old challenging
coat right on his grotesque back.

Quest smiled thinly. 'What's been said is said I guess.'

'What are you, some kind of damn' philosopher?' demanded Elias.

It seemed appropriate then that Judge Cracker should enter the kitchen of Doc's place where the two men had lit down while the old medico got on with his duties.

They didn't know whether he'd heard anything or not, and his remark now was kind of ambiguous.

'Shooting already? You got brain damage or something. Obe?'

'He's too ornery to have brain damage,' said Elias.

'It wasn't me doin' no shootin', old-timer,' said Quest. 'And that little thing is all taken care of now.'

He went past the old man to the door. 'I'll go see how Buck is doing.'

'You do just that, bucko.'

Buck Beckon was sitting up in bed. 'How's the arm?' he asked.

'Fine, thanks.' Quest had it loosely in the sling again but didn't look as if he needed that. 'How are you?'

'I'm fine too. The doc says I'm gonna be all right, Obe.'

Quest sat on the chair beside the bed and looked hard at his cousin, remembering the boy who had been like a brother to him. Buck returned the gaze without flinching.

Obe said, 'There's still somep'n I don't know.
When you were in that card game at the Golden
Palace were you cheating?'

'You gonna arrest me, Obe?'

'Answer my question.'

'I was cheating. But so was that feller called
Jeff. And he wasn't as good at it as I was.'

'Not so good with a gun either it seems.'

'I've been practising.'

'Do tell. So you're gonna try me now, huh?'

'Hell, Obe, you'd plug me before I could get my
gun outa the sheath. You're faster then Earp,
faster then Holliday, Curly Bill or the Kid; faster
than anybody I've ever seen and I've been much
around the gamblin' boys an' the shooters for
years. I know! That's why I ran. But I'm all
through running now.'

Quest smiled thinly. 'You ain't much fixed for
running now.'

'No. But Doc has hopes for me, so maybe I will
be.'

'I hope you will,' said Quest. He made for the
door.

'So long, brother,' said the man in the bed. 'Take
care.'

'So long, brother.' An answer. Softly, as the door
closed.

That night Quest went, for the first time, to his
room at the millinery shop. Homely. Good bed
with soft sheets. Who else had stayed here? But
really now there was no conflict of any kind in his
mind, come what may.

Elias Slack had checked the blockhouse, the prisoners, had two of his boys watching the place, turn and turn about. Nobody had bothered them. Elias and his boys were doing great. Obe knew it, and Elias knew he knew it. They were still partners, had always played it that way.

An argumentative, aggressive, almost don't-give-a-damn attitude which they used to cloak something deeper, stronger.

It was good to be with Elias again. And Elias more maybe than anybody now knew – well, almost – what Obe aimed to do and wouldn't interfere too much. Just a leetle maybe, *just a leetle.*

Della came to Obe that night and they made love. She knew what he must do and didn't try to dissuade him. She understood him greatly, he thought. It was a prime thing to find a woman like that.

But after the tenderness he had to be blunt, tell her straight what he wanted her to do.

'I want you and Polly to go away from here early in the morning.'

'But why, Obe? I want to be with you.'

'Just for a short while, no more'n a day or less. You've got friends out on the ranches, haven't you?'

'Why, yes.' Della was understanding, quick. 'Polly has an aunt and uncle who run a little spread. They're getting old. The old lady is sickly and Polly visits her quite often. We don't both have to be in the shop all the while.'

'Go there then. Will Polly fall in with that?'
'I'm sure she will. If that's the way you want it.'
'That's the way I want it.'
'All right.'

20

It was very quiet and they were sleeping. It was Della who woke the tall man who lay beside her, breathing gently, peacefully. 'Obe.' Nudging him. 'Obe, did you hear that?'

'What?' He was quickly awake, sitting up before she did.

The bedclothes fell away from her nakedness, her breasts softly gleaming in the moonlight that filtered through the window, and a balmy breeze.

'A shot. I'm sure I heard a shot. Muffled, as if indoors. But a shot.'

He slid out of bed, as naked as she was, a fine figure of a man. She joined him, wrapping herself in the sheet, sudden shyness overtaking her.

'Which direction?' he asked.

She pointed, a bit uncertain now, wordless.

'You stay here, honey, hear me?'

'Yes.'

'I'll go take a look.'

Pants on, boots, gunbelt. He was catlike going down the stairs, out through the kitchen to the back door, out on to the back of the sleeping town, taking the direction that Della had indicated.

He remembered Ike Bernet's place, Ike's trouble, though he wasn't sure why that hit him now. But he was by Ike's back door when Ike's woman staggered through.

He moved to her, thinking at first that she was hurt.

She opened her mouth as if to scream, and then she saw him, recognized him.

'I've shot Ike,' she whispered, her eyes wide, staring.

'Go in.'

She moved like an automaton. There was moonlight through the kitchen window. But not enough light. It was Quest who found the lamp on a side shelf and lit it. The woman was motionless, staring at the floor. Quest saw the gun on the kitchen table and picked it up. Warmth came from it.

Ike lay flat on his back on the floor, his face covered with blood.

'He started on me in the bedroom,' the woman said, by rote, as if speaking new words she'd been taught at school. 'He had his belt. He said he was goin' to beat the wickedness out of me. He caught me a few licks but I managed to get down here.'

He saw that she had on only her shift, her feet bare.

'He was raving then. I thought he was goin' to beat me to death. I remembered the gun in the table drawer and I got it out. I just wanted to

scare him off, Mr Quest, I swear. But the gun
went off in my hand....'

By then Quest was on one knee before Ike who
was still alive. Quest still had the gun, said,
'You're lucky you didn't blow your head off. This
weapon doesn't look as if it's been cleaned for
years, let alone fired. It certainly shouldn't have
been left loaded.'

'It went off,' parroted the woman.

'The slug just creased his forehead,' said Quest.
'You were lucky, both o' you I guess. Go fetch Doc
Keane.'

'Yes. Yes.' She went through the back door.
There was a male voice out there. Quest put the
old gun on the kitchen table and drew his own
weapon.

But it was only one of Elias's boys who said he
thought he'd heard a shot. 'An accident,' said
Quest. 'A gun went off. Will you see that that lady
gets to the doc. I'll stay here.'

When the doc and the woman appeared Ike was
beginning to moan.

The little, plump medico was quick. 'I'll
bandage him,' he said. 'He'll have a headache for
days an' he won't be able to fight his friend Jack
any more. You go back to bed, Obe.'

Obe did what he was told. He reassured Della.
They made love again and they slept. They were
both awake early in the morning, and so was
Polly. The girls had always been early risers.

They had a smart little gig with a trotting
horse. From the back window Quest watched

them until they disappeared from his sight in the burgeoning morning sun.

He went back into the full of the house which seemed very empty. He was a natural loner. But he didn't think he had ever felt so alone before.

The town of Lobo Forks was coming awake now, and he had to be out there.

But first he went to the undertaker's, Petey's place.

When he came out of there he was carrying something.

He was a strong man, didn't need any help.

21

He placed his burden in the middle of Main Street just a little way back from the entrance to the Dirty Ace Saloon.

A corpse lashed to the kitchen chair, sitting upright and staring.

The corpse of Derry Saxe, young, reckless, not too sensible or keen; very dead.

And the tall man standing beside what had once been Derry. A tall man with a silver star shining on his breast. The new marshal.

The new marshal they had all heard of and were expecting something from. And now they were about to get something it seemed.

A show. *A show-up*. A climax; and a denouement.

And the voice rising. Not a bull-voice, but a resounding, clear one, a clarion call.

'Cal Beaucaire. Do you hear me, Cal Beaucaire? Come out here an' take a last look at your friend before he's buried.'

The shifting forms. The morning street emptying.

Man and corpse alone. Waiting.

There was unseen movement though. More movement than could possibly have met the eye of anybody.

Had this been expected? Some folks thought it had.

A man with a rifle behind a curtain in a window heard a voice grate in his ear.

'Lower it slowly, buster.'

And the rifle being taken slowly by a big hand and then a gun descending, a gun-barrel bringing oblivion to the rifleman.

A young man in an alley with a gun in each hand turning suddenly, but not suddenly enough, meeting a driving fist to the jaw – a beautiful blow placed by an expert – and hitting the hard ground in a senseless heap, lying still while a grinning pugilist even younger than himself collected the twin guns and pushed them into his own belt.

A man with a knife – not all the marshal's back-up were pugilists – threatening a barfly with a shot-gun, taking it from him and clouting him alongside the head with it.

Two men held at bay in the saloon. Two more coming out of the Golden Palace – though there had been no all-night session there – and running into another man with a shot-gun. Backing. Shepherded, threatened with extinction, shucking their shining Colts.

A man waving from a rooftop.

And that echoing voice calling again.

'Cal Beaucaire! Come out, Cal Beaucaire, come out an' meet a corpse.'

And the echoes dying. And only the silence. As if all the town was as dead as the corpse seated in the sun, and the corpse's keeper, tall and as shining as an avenging angel in the sun, was all that was left.

But then somebody said 'He's coming', and it was like a whisper that went from mouth to mouth.

Obadiah Quest stepped away from the side of his dead companion but did not move forward, just stood still then, stood and waited.

Beaucaire was a big man with long arms. He carried his guns low and he wore a pair of them, Colt Peacemakers in long holsters which had once held very heavy Dragoons until their owner had changed them.

He had only killed one man yet with the Peacemakers. They were pretty fine guns.

But Cal had always hedged his bets anyway, covered himself.

'Move,' he said. 'Move, damn you.'

He wanted this man to show something; to get blasted. The son-of-a-bitch was still as a post, didn't move, didn't even answer.

Quest had shucked his sling last night. That arm was still stiff and he hoped he wouldn't have to use it. He noted that Beaucaire toted twin guns. But that didn't faze him none! He had his Smith and Wesson in its usual holster.

He'd had that gun modified to suit him,

including a filing down of the trigger. He could snap off shots pretty good with the hammer.

He had taken his stubby Bulldog pistol from the back of his belt and now wore it in his side, the opposite side from the S & W.

The sun was slanting now. It was not directly shining into the eyes of either of the two men.

The third man was sitting staring. He seemed to be grinning.

Beaucaire was moving forward, as if impelled to do so. But very slowly.

Quest didn't think there was any uncertainty about that, though.

Quest was long since all through shouting, making his sardonic show-off play, goading his man.

'Make your play, Marshal,' said Beaucaire.

Was he mocking now?

He didn't dare look from left to right.

He came closer, and then he stopped.

There was nobody in sight except the two men and the corpse. Unseen eyes watched and a town held its breath.

Make your play! But Beaucaire was all through waiting, his wide shoulders sloping lower, his long arms just right, just there, clawed hands poised over walnut butts of guns.

The right hand just a little bit faster than the left.

It had seemed, with Beaucaire, that there was just a tiny suggestion of a crouch. But Quest was still upright, his arm seemingly lax. But his right hand curled, grasped, came up with the shining gun and the arm straightened out and the barrel was levelled.

It seemed that at least two guns spoke at the same time....

He was a wild kid. His new boss, Beaucaire had told him what to do and he was very eager. He wanted to step out and blast down the tall, arrogant, shouting man with the silver badge on his chest. He peeped around his corner and shifted his feet impatiently.

He didn't hear anything of the slippered feet behind him. Pecos George moved very lightly for so bulky a man.,

'Brother,' said George.

'Oh,' said the man and he turned, his gun coming up.

George hit him across the side of the head, a swinging blow with axe-handle, shiny and new from George's own well-appointed store.

There was a soft 'clunk'.

But the kid fell without a sound.

Crip wasn't as pugnacious as George. He certainly didn't take any chances. But the little man with the baby-blue eyes could move as silently as an angel.

He brought his man down with a blow to the back of the head from the barrel of a Colt that he had never used in anger before. Like a limp, badly filled sack of grain, the man fell against him. But Crip was able to hold him, lower him.

Another culprit. Another alley.

Crip laughed in a whisper.

He and Pecos George – although they couldn't actually see each other – both watched the street now.

Beaucaire. Quest.

Quest. Beaucaire.

But it was Beaucaire who staggered as his second gun went off a breath of a moment after the first one and the shot whined away into nothingness.

And even the first shot hadn't been straight and true. Or maybe Quest had moved a fraction to one side as he drew. His first movement. He could have crouched a little.... Both men were so fast that the action had seemed frenetic, explosive.

As the gunshots echoed like drumbeats in the distance.

But, then again, Quest's action had been a mite smoother, a mite faster, more than a mite more accurate.

Beaucaire was staggering backwards, teetering on his heels, a bullet in his chest, a red gleaming stain already on his shirtfront. He was trying to lift his guns again, though the first smoking one that he'd fired, the left-hand one, was way down. He was trying to lift this, and it was like an anvil, and even the other gun wasn't level, when Quest's second bullet hit him, no more than a couple of inches from the first one. And he was driven back

as if he'd been hit by an invisible fist and his heels
left the ground and he tilted. Then his shoulders
hit the ground, his head.

He kicked like a toad, and then he flattened,
spreadeagled. He was still. And there was then
what seemed like a great sigh, though it was from
nowhere, *seemed from nowhere*.

A bullet hit the ground at Obadiah Quest's feet,
spitting dust. He fell to one knee, leaning
sideways a bit, gun lifted, hat askew, red-gold
hair shining in the sun. Looking upwards,
squinting.

A man's figure limned against the sun on a
rooftop.

Quest's gun speaking again and the man jerked
so that he seemed to be dancing like a broken doll,
a marionette whose strings were broken, a
chicken with a blood-soaked head.

There had been a strange echo.

'A rifleshot,' some wiseacre said.

And another man was standing on another
rooftop and waving to the tall man below.

A smoking rifle. And Elias 'Mad Boy' Slack
saying aloud to himself, 'Christ, we almost missed
that one.'

But, at last, the bushwhacker had not been
missed. Quest's bullet from his handgun had hit
the man squarely in the forehead. Elias's
rifle-slug had hit him almost simultaneously in
the side of the head.

The man had quit dancing. He was out of sight
now.

Oh, he'd been well-hidden all right, waiting for Quest to move forward to meet Beaucaire, waiting for a clean shot, hadn't got a really good one after all, should've picked his position better. And Quest hadn't moved worth a damn – and the feller had had to show himself.

His relaxing muscles must have twitched or something. He rolled. Somebody cried out in shock as the body plummeted from the roof, out of nothingness it seemed.

Then the dead feller, with most of his head missing, lay in a mess of blood and dust in the middle of Main Street not far from the corpse of the man who'd set him up for this.

Obadiah Quest stood laxly, gun sheathed, long arms hanging.

Folks came forward.

They carried away two bodies. And a man in a chair, also dead. The undertaker waited at his door.

Disgruntled drygulchers were being shepherded towards incarceration in the blockhouse, the improvised jail of Lobo Forks. Some of them had to be helped along or roughly half-carried.

Elias Slack joined the marshal in the sun.

Neither of them said anything for a bit. They began to walk slowly.

Then Quest said, 'I'll get my horse.'

'A ride will do you good,' Elias said.

They ambled.

'You need company?'

'No, thanks, *amigo*. But tell me, do you know

where the little spread is where Miss Polly's aunt an' uncle hang out?'

'Sure.' Elias pointed out at the edge of town. 'Take the main trail. When it forks take the right-hand thin track. It'll lead you right to the place. Brown barn there, you'll see it in the sun.'

Soon he watched the tall man ride out, not turning to wave.